"I'll tell you wl  learned he was abs and again. You think you've finished ...

"Like the Princess Paulownia tree," she cut in. She closed the book distractedly and returned it to the drawer.

"Princess what?" he asked with a tilt of his head.

"There was this tree or maybe it was a weed—I was never sure. It came up year after year, no matter how often Daddy chopped it down. He'd hack it down to the ground on one side of the porch, and it'd pop up on the other. The roots just wouldn't let go."

"That was exactly my professor's point. In families, predispositions of the darkest kind recede, then surface again. That's just the way he said it, *recede, then surface again.* You'd never think, and then suddenly..." He paced away from the counter and, rounding the gurney, came to a stop in the center of the room. "Dr. McGinnis, you realize that if not for the murder of the last remaining Bilyeu—"

"—who was an innocent."

"A sacrificial lamb, just trying to set things right."

"Very sad." She locked the drawer and slipped the key into her lab coat pocket.

"Well, I'd like to finish the job," he said.

"By finding the murderer of John Doe?"

He nodded.

"I wonder if the perpetrator is still alive." She stood before the skeleton, looking not at the hands or the ribs where dagger had met bone, but at the skull, the hollow cavities where eyes had once been.

The Summer House at Larkspur

by

Kay Pritchett

Mosey Frye Mysteries, Book 4

The Summer House at Larkspur

Cover Art by *Kristian Norris*

The Wild Rose Press, Inc.
PO Box 708
Adams Basin, NY 14410-0708
Visit us at www.thewildrosepress.com

Publishing History
First Edition, 2023
Trade Paperback ISBN 978-1-5092-4564-2
Digital ISBN 978-1-5092-4565-9

Mosey Frye Mysteries, Book 4
Published in the United States of America

Dedication

For Chris

Chapter One

Tuesday, September 22, late afternoon
Hermitage, St. Mary of the Angels Church

A short distance from the threshold of the hermitage, Sister Clare lay flat of her back, staring up at the sky. Overhead, a thin layer of clouds drifted slowly eastward. A pair of dark birds—crows, vultures, or turkey hawks— glided across the emblazoned wash of blue. Sister Clare, her eyes fixed, appeared undisturbed by the bright rays of the sun, though the heavens fairly dazzled with early autumn light.

Her cat Grim Milly Grimalkin popped up from a robust patch of sunflowers and crept toward her mistress, then gently pawed her ashen face. When Sister Clare didn't respond, Grim Milly bumped her gray, wooly head against her mistress's cheek.

A truck rumbled down the road and screeched to a halt. At the sound of brakes, the cat skittered away. Two men and a boy dressed in light-weight hunting gear stepped down from the cab. "What's the bag limit, Frank Jr.?" the elder of the two men said.

"No limit," the driver answered.

"You sure 'bout that?"

Frank Jr. confirmed with a dip of his chin.

The third member of the group, a lanky adolescent, pulled a cell phone from his pants pocket and tapped the screen. " 'Mourning doves,' " he read aloud, " 'bag limit fifteen. Eurasian collared-doves, bag limit forty-five.' "

The older man, the one who had posed the question, reached into the back of the truck for a paper bag and shook it close to the ground. Small corpses spilled out, fouling the air with the smell of gunpowder and fresh blood. He picked up two birds and pitched them toward his son's bag. "Frank Jr., you take two of these."

"Hang on, Papa," the adolescent said. " 'Doves the hunter gives to another *must* be accompanied by written and signed information stating the number of birds being transferred.' "

His grandfather chuckled. "As I was saying, Frank Jr., you take two. I'm over limit."

The boy, who was called Sonny, slipped the phone into his pocket and, picking up his shotgun, waggled it mischievously in the direction of his grandfather, who'd squatted to gather up the day's bounty.

"Sonny, stop that," Frank Jr. said. "A rifle is not a toy." He shook a finger at his son, then reached down and plucked two doves off the ground.

Grim Milly, lured by the scent of fresh game, came out of her hiding place beneath a juniper. The youngest hunter, spotting the cat, raised his weapon to his shoulder. He rested his cheek against the stock and pointed the barrel.

"Sonny Boy, stop, fool!" his father shouted. "That's Sister Clare's cat."

He lowered his gun. "I wasn't going to kill it."

"Yeah, I *bet* you weren't." Frank Jr. hurled his cap at Grim Milly. "Scat! Get out of here."

But Milly stood her ground, reticent to abandon the display of dead birds.

"Scat!" he repeated.

She darted back toward her mistress.

Frank Sr. grabbed a piece of newspaper from the truck bed and wrapped the birds. "I'm takin' a couple of these to Sister Clare," he said, then plodded off toward the hermitage. But as soon as he rounded the patch, he stopped. "Sister Clare, is that you? Hey, it's Frank." He hastened his step. "Sister Clare, are you okay? I got some doves for you."

Sister Clare didn't move.

He reached her and, dropping to his knees, pressed his fingers against her throat. "God! Oh, my God!" He stood and called to his son, "Frank, get over here."

"What is it, Daddy?" Frank Jr. chucked his sack in the truck bed and circled the patch.

"She's dead," the older man said, the color drained from his face.

Back at the truck, the boy called out, "Daddy, what's wrong?" He approached, then stopped near the body.

"She's gone, Sonny," Frank Jr. said. "Sister Clare's gone."

"Papa," Sonny said, "you got blood all over you."

Frank Sr. got to his feet and looked down at his pants legs, soaked from knee to hem in the dead woman's blood. He unbuckled his straps, let his outer gear fall to the ground. "Sonny, hand me a pair of pants out of the back of the truck, would you?"

Frank Sr. changed his pants and tucked in his shirt. "I've got to get over to the church, see if anybody's there." He started down the path, then called back, "Frank, call the police. Ask for Lieutenant Olivera. Tell him to get over to St. Mary's Church quick as he can."

Frank Jr. nodded and reached for his phone.

Kay Pritchett

"Tell him Sister Clare's dead."

Chapter Two

The coroner pulled her SUV into the clearing behind Frank's truck, stepped out, and retrieved a camera and instrument case from the back.

"Young McGinnis." Frank Sr. shoved his hands into his pockets.

"Mr. Ferguson," she said, "Lieutenant Olivera's on his way. He and Springer are out on Little Smith. They'll be here soon as they can."

"Glad you were close by." He looked sheepishly at Dr. McGinnis. "We haven't touched anything. Well, I checked for a pulse," he corrected. "She was dead when we got here—me and Frank Jr. and Sonny." He signaled in the direction of his son and grandson, who were sitting on a pair of stone benches in the shade of a chinaberry. "Then I went to get Father Moody." He gestured toward the priest.

Moody pushed ahead of the coroner and knelt by the corpse. He drew a small bottle from his breast pocket and began to anoint the body.

"Father Moody," Dr. McGinnis said, throwing out a hand. "I can't allow you to compromise the crime scene. Please…"

He looked askance at the coroner and went on with

5

his ritual.

"Father Moody, you're flushed." Frank Sr. touched him on the arm. "Why don't you sit over yonder with Frank and Sonny."

The priest complied, and Dr. McGinnis moved in. She took photographs from various angles and, propping herself on one hand and bended knees, leaned over the body. "Stab wound, looks like, judging by the state of the corpse."

"Yeah," Frank Sr. said, "that's what I thought."

"Tremendous loss of blood," she continued, "but I'll know more when I've finished the autopsy." She stood, scanned the surrounding area, then pulled off her gloves and took a recording device from her pocket. "Middle-aged female, identified as Sister Clare."

"She been dead long?" Frank Sr. said.

"Hmm, not too long, but in this heat it's hard to say. An hour or two, maybe." She stepped warily around the body. "No sign of a weapon, footprints in the area of the corpse."

A police van roared up and came to a halt alongside the coroner's SUV. Two men got out.

Grim Milly, who'd befriended Sonny, wiggled free of his hold and returned to her spot under the juniper.

A man dressed in uniform opened the back of the van and began pulling out orange cones. The other, tall, slender, wearing a straw Fedora and linen sports jacket, walked up quickly. "Dr. McGinnis."

"Lieutenant Olivera." She nodded, then went on speaking into the recorder.

Olivera paused for a moment, biting his lip. "Careful with the cones, Springer. Look out for footprints." He backed away from the body and walked toward the clearing where the vehicles were parked. "Frank, Father Moody, over here, please." He motioned with his hand. "Let's not disturb the crime scene any more than it has been."

Frank Sr. walked toward Olivera. "Sorry, we didn't know. If we'd known, well, we didn't. We got out of the truck, me, Frank Jr., and Sonny, and, uh…"

Olivera pulled a tablet and pen from his breast pocket and leaned against the front of the van. "I'm going to want all of you to come down to the station for prints and a cheek swab." His penetrating eyes flicked from one man to the next and came to rest on Sonny Ferguson. "The boy, too."

"A cheek swab," the priest repeated.

"DNA evidence. Springer's going to take your outer clothing and shoes and give you something to put on."

Father Moody rubbed his hands against his blood-soiled slacks. "If I could go to the rectory—"

"Sorry, Father," Springer cut in, "we need to gather all the evidence we can, so we can sort out—"

"Springer," Olivera said, "the yellow tape, if you don't mind."

"Right, Chief."

"Let me start with you, Frank. Tell me exactly what happened."

The men formed a semicircle in front of Olivera, while Sonny, cell phone in hand, perched on a big rock at the edge of the clearing.

"As I was saying before," Frank Sr. began, "we'd been hunting in a thicket, oh, 'bout a quarter mile from here. We pulled up in the clearing to divvy up the birds."

"What time was that?"

Frank Sr. glanced toward the boy. "Sonny, what

time was it?"

"Four-thirty, 'bout," he replied.

Olivera turned to Sonny. "You sure?"

"Yes, sir. I looked at my phone." He held his phone up for Olivera to see.

"So, the three of you pulled up here about four-thirty, parked your truck, got out—"

"That's right," Frank Sr. said.

"Any reason in particular?"

"We always stop here in the clearing. I take Sister Clare a couple of birds, then, uh, head home from here."

Frank Jr. spoke up. "It's not every day, Lieutenant, we stumble on a body."

"I guess not." Olivera cleared his throat. "And you just happened to see Sister Clare?"

"I didn't," Frank Jr. said, "but my daddy did."

"Soon as I came 'round that patch of sunflowers," Frank Sr. said, "I seen her lying there, just like that." He pointed toward the body. "I called to her. She didn't answer. I called again. Then I walked over there and, uh, saw the blood." His voice broke. "She was dead."

"And you and your son?" Olivera said to Frank Jr.

"I was waiting for Daddy by the truck, but when he told me to get over there—"

"How close did you get? Did you touch the body?"

"Close, but I didn't touch nothin'."

"And your son—where was he?"

"By the truck...till we seen her lying there. Then, uh, when Daddy left to go to the church, Sonny and me, we sat down over there on the benches."

"Father Moody, when did you arrive?"

Father Moody took a step toward Olivera. "Frank came to the rectory. Not sure what time it was exactly.

Before five," he said, nodding, "yeah, a little before five. I was about to fix a bite to eat. He told me Sister Clare was dead." He pulled out his handkerchief and wiped his nose. "I came back with Frank. I tried to administer last rights, but Dr. McGinnis—"

"You touched the body, Father?"

"No, I don't believe I did. I knelt beside her."

"I see. You didn't touch the body, but you knelt beside the body." Olivera made a note. "One more thing." He tapped his pad. "I don't suppose any of you saw anyone who could have been the assailant—anyone driving away, walking through the woods?"

Frank Jr. shook his head in bewilderment. "No, we didn't meet nobody, not driving, not walking."

"And you, Frank Sr., you didn't see anyone between here and the church? Didn't hear anything?"

The eldest Ferguson rubbed his chin. "I don't think I did, but, uh, to be honest, I don't know *what* I saw or *what* I heard."

"Did you know the deceased?"

"I've known her since she was a baby."

"Father Moody, did you see anyone in or near the church?"

"No one, not since mass this morning."

"Did you see or speak with the deceased?"

"Not since mass."

"Did she mention anything that, uh, struck you as different, peculiar?"

"No." Moody shook his head.

"If you think of anything, anything at all." Olivera slipped his pad in his pocket, then addressed the coroner. "Dr. McGinnis, are you finished with the preliminaries?"

She nodded.

"When might I expect your report?"

A timid smile crossed her face. "That depends."

"On what?" His eyes softened.

"The tests I need to run." Turning away, she ducked into the trunk of her vehicle and pulled out a body bag. "Sergeant, could you help me with this, please?"

As soon as the coroner had departed with the corpse and Springer had bagged the bloodstained garments and shoes, Olivera brought his initial interview to a halt. "I need to see all of you tomorrow morning first thing."

"Lieutenant Olivera," Father Moody said, "I have mass in the morning."

"We're harvesting," Frank Jr. said. "We gotta be in the field by daybreak."

"You understand we're dealing with a murder," Olivera said calmly.

"Yeah," Frank Sr. said, "but we could meet a little later in the day, couldn't we?"

"Sorry, Frank."

Once the witnesses departed, Olivera, with Springer at his heels, headed toward the hermitage. He paused mid-path to look at Father Moody as he moved along the foot trail to the church.

"Springer," Olivera said, "that trail has got to be searched thoroughly, but first—"

"Chief, look at that," Springer cut in.

A prop plane roared overhead.

"That's strange." He peered up through the boughs of the chinaberry. The plane had left a thin stream of smoke in the shape of a cross over the spot where, moments before, the dead nun had lain.

"It must have flown from north to south," Springer said, "then east to west. Huh."

"What time is it?" Olivera said.

Springer glanced down at his watch. "Getting onto six."

"Call the control tower. Let's see if we can get the name of the pilot."

Springer did as Olivera said and got a name. "Cecil DeGroat's his name, Chief. But he was a tad off his flight plan."

"Destination?"

"New Orleans."

"Get his license number—and address and phone, if you can."

Chapter Three

Tuesday, September 22, 4:00 p.m.
Shepherd Realty, Hembree

Saffron Smiley sat in the light of the late afternoon sun and, from her desk near the window, squinted at the boarded up gas station across the street. The Hog Blog calendar on the wall above her desk confirmed that fall had come at last to Hembree. But Guy MacAfee's big thermometer across at the station told a different story, its vein of ethanol steadily pushing its meniscus upward toward the end of the expansion bulb.

Hembree folk were hard-pressed to take the slightest note of summer's passing, if not for the whirring and crackling of the mechanical pickers in the fields and the comings and goings of trailers loaded with big, round bales. The cotton bales of recent times—or "modules" as they call them now—looked not a bit like the old-timey square bales that, between field and gin yard, made a show of their fluffy, white commodity. Present-day cotton exited the fields as stocky cylinders packaged in plastic casings. Divested of natural dignity, cotton had nothing left to flaunt. Except, of course, for the lucre it guaranteed the entrepreneurs who planted, harvested, and ginned it, before shipping it off by train, truck, or barge, to North Carolina or China.

Saffron had stepped away from her desk to

photocopy an ad, when an out-of-the-ordinary young man hesitantly entered the front office of Shepherd Realty. Tall and thin as a willow, he had a youthful face, handsome but ruggedly formed. From under a mouse-colored hat, which sat perfectly level on his head, came a bounty of chestnut hair that fell in corkscrews to his shoulders. He wore a gray plaid shirt with the shirttail out, a brown wool sweater tied loosely around his waist, and, on his feet, high-top boots—not especially stylish but of a fine quality all the same. He was carrying a canvas backpack with a goat hide pouch that dangled from the bottom. He unclipped the pouch, unscrewed the stopper, and, tilting his head back, poured a stream of water into his mouth.

"May I help you?" Saffron said. She duplicated the page from the *Hembree Shopper* and tacked the copy on the bulletin board. Settled in her chair again, she inspected the young man from hat to boots, boots to hat, pausing in each direction to frown unabashedly at his hair.

"Actually—" he began.

"Mm-hmm."

"—I want to speak to one of your agents."

Her eyebrows rose, then dropped into a slight frown. "That would be Ms. Mosey Frye. Let me see if she's available. May I ask your name?"

"Rafael de Lobos."

"You're going to have to spell that for me." As he spelled, she printed the letters on a small yellow note pad, then said, as she pointed with her pompadour toward a row of chairs, "Take a seat. I'll tell her you're here." She wedged her way out of her cubbyhole and, without a knock, entered the agent's office. "You have a visitor." She stifled a snort. "His name is Rafael de Lobos." She laid the note on the desk.

Mosey reached for it. "Da what?"

"Rafael de Lobos," she said and, with a disparaging shake of her head, started out the door.

"Fine. Send him in."

Mosey stood up, stretched her arms over her head, and yawned. Her eyes traveled to a digital clock on the wall. September 22, first day of fall. She picked up a brown envelope from a pile of forms and, fanning herself, walked to the window and snapped the shutters to a half-closed position.

"You are Ms. Frye?"

She cocked her head, more puzzled at the young man's appearance than his accent. "I'm Ms. Frye, but you can call me Mosey—everybody does. Come on in, won't you?"

"Yes, thank you," he said.

"Have a seat."

He unbuckled the strap from around his waist and balanced his pack against the wall. Then, untying the sleeves of his sweater, he draped it over the pack.

"Were you referred?" She returned to her desk.

"No, I saw the sign, Shepherd Realty." He sat in the chair across from Mosey, removed his hat, and placed it on his knees.

She eyed the young man's dusty boots. "You hitch here?"

"Oh, no, miss. I came by plane."

"Where from?"

"New York City. I changed planes in New York City. I am a Spaniard. You say Spaniard or Spanish?"

"I say—" She paused. What *did* she say? "Either

14

one, I guess, but Spanish is more common."

"I am from Sevilla. You say Seville, I believe."

"That's right." She leaned forward and looked into his hazel eyes. "Rafael de—"

"—de Lobos." He fanned his face with his hat and set it back on his knees. "It's *castellano*."

"*Castellano*," she repeated with a slight Italian accent.

"You speak *castellano*?" His face beamed with expectancy.

"Not really. I speak Italian, but I can make out a little *castellano*."

"Oh, yes, they are similar. I can make out, as you say, a little *italiano* and a little *portugués*."

"*Portugués*," she repeated, again with a cadence proper to the only language other than English she spoke with a degree of fluency.

"You speak *portugués*?" he said.

"No, English and some Italian."

"Well, if you like, I can teach you Spanish."

"That's certainly nice of you to offer. It'd come in handy around here these days." She pushed back and swiveled. "But I was thinking I could do something for *you*. You must be looking for a house, an apartment?"

"Yes, that is true. I am looking for a place."

"To buy, to rent?"

"Not to buy, not to rent."

"Then?" She stopped swiveling.

He stretched toward his pack and pulled out a piece of parchment, unfolded it with care, and placed it on her desk. "This," he said, as he tapped insistently on a spot near the center of the quaint document, "I want to find this place."

"May I see?"

"Careful. The *plano* is old." He lifted the parchment with both hands and held it up for her to see.

"*Plano*? What is this—an old map, a pictograph?"

"Map of a town."

"This is a map of—"

"This town, Hembree, Arkansas," he said.

"Hembree. Goodness gracious, this is a very old *plano*."

"Yes, very old. My *bisabuelo*, father of my father's father—"

"Great-grandfather."

"Yes, my great-grandfather drew this map from memory. He gave it to his son, my grandfather."

Mosey took a close look at the drawing. It didn't look like any map she'd ever seen, except maybe for a period map in a history book. There wasn't any ocean, of course, with mythical creatures staring up from the water. But, yes, there was a pond, rounder than any pond she could think of in Hembree. And right out in the middle, there was a flat-bottom boat with blue-green boards outlined in black ink. Near the pond, stood a house, a tall, narrow house with a slanted roof. Each roof tile was distinctly traced, just like the boards of the boat. She looked up. "What an amazing map. You say your great-grandfather drew it?"

"Yes, from memory, as I said. My father told me that."

"Well, if you ask me, he was quite a cartographer."

"Cartog—"

"Map maker."

"Yes, *cartógrafo*. My great-grandfather was a—"

"Car-to-gra-pher."

He repeated it several times until "cartographer" rolled off his tongue as if English were his native language.

"But your great-grandfather," she said, "surely he didn't come to Hembree. Hembree isn't all that old." She calculated. "How old *is* your great-grandfather?"

"He died."

"But how old *would* he be if he were alive?"

"He was born early in the past century…1900, about then."

"I see. Well, maybe he *did* know Hembree." His great-grandfather, after all, must have been about the age of her grandfather, who had come to Hembree in the mid-twenties, not many years before the torrential waters of the Mississippi had sent every resident scurrying for high ground.

"He came here as a young man," he said. "There was a dictatorship in Spain, and he left the country. He found work here and stayed a few years till the dictator was thrown out, ex—how do you say?"

"Exiled."

"Yes, exiled."

"Not Franco?"

"No, not Franco. The *Generalísimo*, he came later. José Antonio Primo de Rivera."

She stopped to admire the pleasant trill with which her visitor pronounced "Rivera."

"What did you say his name was?"

"José Antonio Primo de Rivera."

She strained to remember her European history but could recall no such person. "So, your great-grandfather must have been—"

"*Republicano*. He fought in the Spanish Civil War,

fought for the Re—"

"Republic. Get rid of king," she suggested in clipped English.

"Yes. He was in the government. They killed him."

"Oh, that is—"

"—tragic, very tragic, but that happened a long time ago. Spain is free now. No more dictator."

She shifted her gaze from her visitor to the map, then to the backpack that had toppled onto the floor.

"And you have come here to…"

His answer wasn't immediate. He looked at her and then reached for the map. "I need to find this house."

"Well, that might be difficult. An older house, it could be standing, I suppose. I could look. Might I see that again?"

He passed her the map, and she picked it up and walked to the window for better light. She pushed back the shutters and examined the map's peculiar structures and conduits. On the left side—not in the middle where one would expect to find the town center—she spotted a square, lined with tall, leafy trees. "This could be the Square," she voiced softly, "and if it is, then this building must be the courthouse, and this, the Tavernette. Uh-huh, I think I'm starting to make sense of your map, Rafael. May I call you Rafael?"

"Certainly," he said with a nod. "What do you see?"

She laid the parchment in front of him. "I see the main square. Right here." She tapped on the parchment. "This has to be the courthouse and this, the Tavernette."

"Tavernette?"

"That's what we call it. It's a very old tavern."

"Yes, *taberna* we say. A pub," he said brightly, pronouncing the "u" like the "oo" in "moo."

"Pub," she corrected. "Like an English pub."

"Or a Spanish pub."

"You have pubs?"

"Oh, yes, there are many pubs in Seville."

"Well, in Hembree we only have one pub, and that's the Tavernette, right there." She tapped again.

They examined the area between the Square and the pond. Given the inexactness of the map's dimensions and layout, she could only guess that the pond was situated somewhere northeast of the Square. There were streets and roads, all tree-lined. Lamentably, none bore a name. Rooftops with clearly penned shingles jutted out from the trees. A lone structure appeared here and there, and an occasional chicken or pig peeked out from behind a porch post. A horse, not much larger than the pigs, jumped a fence. A small herd of spotted cows grazed in an apple-green field a stone's throw from the Tavernette. The landscape, shown in green for the most part, was broken up by a kidney-shaped pond on the upper right and a winding stream on the lower left. A pair of dapple-gray mules with braided manes and tails waded into the stream for a drink.

"Rafael," Mosey said, "would you mind terribly if I made a copy of your map?"

"Copy?"

"A photocopy. It won't hurt it. I'll be careful."

"No problem."

"I'll just be a second."

As she left the room, she glanced back. He was watching her but quickly diverted his focus back to the spot where the map had lain.

Chapter Four

Tuesday, September 22, 4:30 p.m.
Shepherd Realty

Mosey called the Tavernette to see if they had a vacancy. "It's an easy walk. Go that way." She waved her arm in the direction of the Square. "It's a couple of blocks. You'll see it, sign over the door...Tavernette."

"Thanks, Ms. Frye." Rafael shaded his eyes.

"Mosey, call me Mosey, like I said."

"Mosey, right. I'll be back tomorrow."

"Call first." She handed him a card. "Here's my number."

"Thanks." He unbuttoned a pocket on the backpack and dropped it in, then placed his hat on his head and started off. But at her wave good-bye, he stopped, removed his hat, and returned her gesture with a bow.

She entered the office and paused at Saffron's desk. "What a regal young man."

"Regal!" Saffron harrumphed. She ripped a sheet from her pad and handed it to Mosey. "If you say so."

"Who's this?"

"It says who it is right there."

"A. B. Bilyeu. Is he kin to the Bilyeus around here?"

"I haven't the slightest idea. Call him."

"What about?"

"Didn't say." She lifted her magazine and picked up

a pen. "Give me that."

"This?" Mosey waved the yellow slip.

"That." She grabbed it and added a name. "Call Ms. McCutter over at the office supply. She called yesterday and again this morning."

Mosey read aloud the name at the top of the list. "A. B. Bilyeu." She walked back to her desk and punched in the number.

A mere whimper of a voice said hello.

"Mr. Bilyeu?" she said.

"Yes, this is A. B. Bilyeu. Who's calling?"

"Mosey Frye of Shepherd Realty. Ms. Smiley said you called."

"Oh, yes," he said. "I called just a minute ago. I was hoping you could help me find a place in Hembree or, if not Hembree, nearby. I'm looking for a summer house, nothing too big, mind you. Near water would be good."

"A summer house," she repeated, "and preferably near water."

He coughed and cleared his throat. "That's right."

"But, were you wanting it for now?"

"Soon as possible."

"Would you be interested in a rental or a place to buy?"

"I can't be too particular, given the situation."

"Situation?"

"I need something now. As I said, soon as possible."

"I don't know that I have anything listed that would be exactly what you're looking for, but I'd be happy to check around. You wouldn't happen to be—"

"I'd appreciate that," he cut in. "Can I expect to hear back soon?"

"I'll make it a priority."

"Thank you, ma'am."

"Thank you, sir, and thanks for calling Shepherd Realty." She put down the receiver. "Saffron!"

"What?"

"Summer houses—we got any listings?"

Saffron's head came through the door. "Summer houses in Hembree?"

"Mr. Bilyeu of area code 504—wherever that is—says he's looking for a summer house near water. I tried to ask him if he was related to the Bilyeus, but he cut me off." She picked up the book of listings in the greater Hembree area and started turning pages. "You know of anything that matches that description? And not too big, he said."

"What's he want a summer house for now?"

"I don't know. Maybe he figures the end of the season is the perfect time to buy. Might pick up something at a reduced price. John Earle got anything like that you know of offhand?"

"He's got the old Bilyeu place."

"Huh? Bilyeu place? Now, that's odd. He didn't mention—"

"Well, it's not that odd. It's a fairly common name in south Louisiana."

"Sounds Cajun."

"It is, and I've heard it pronounced Buh-loo, like "skip to Buh-loo." She giggled.

"Buh-loo, then."

"Far as I know," Saffron said, "Sister Clare's the only Bilyeu around here. The rest are long gone."

"Like moved away or dead?"

"Dead."

"And this Sister Clare, you know her?"

"I know *of* her," Saffron said.

"So where is this place?"

"It's off Little Smith, right past the Civil War cemetery. I thought you were born here, Mosey. Never heard of the Bilyeu place, indeed."

"I don't know any place past the Civil War cemetery."

"It's the only one out there."

"What's it look like?"

"Huh," Saffron grunted. "Like a pack of thieves been living in it. It sits way back from the road on the other side of Two Mile Lake. You can barely see it from the road. A row of big, tall cypresses—"

"There's a house back there?" Mosey interrupted.

"Yes, there's a house back there. That's the old Bilyeu place, I'm telling you."

"And it's John Earle's listing?"

"Yes, ma'am."

"You got the specs there handy?"

"It's in that book right in front of you." Saffron turned to the section titled "Lake-front Properties."

"Let me see." Mosey pulled the book from under her nose. "Forty-six thousand. Cheap as dirt. But 1,800 square feet. That might be a little too big for Mr. A. B. Bilyeu."

Turning to leave, Saffron added, "You'd better call John Earle."

"What for?"

"That couple who stopped by this morning—"

"The man and woman from Ebenezer?"

"That's the one. They were asking directions over to the Bilyeu place."

"Do me a favor, would you? Check out the MLS and

take a peek at the Historic Homes."

"I got a better idea," Saffron said, eyebrows raised. "*You* check out the MLS, and I'll take a peek at the Historic Homes." She headed out the door.

"Fine." Mosey wheeled around in her chair to face the illuminated screen of her laptop. Pulling up the most complete listing available of homes for sale in the Hembree area, she typed in the specifications her client had mentioned. "Price...he didn't say anything about price."

"Mosey!"

"Oh, for God's sake, Saffron, stop your yelping, I'm coming."

She found her at the printer, retrieving a sheet of paper, which she handed to Mosey over her shoulder.

"The print's faint. I can hardly read it."

Saffron pounded the machine, pressed the button, and pulled out a second copy.

" 'Summer house,' " Mosey read aloud, " 'Bilyeu estate. Lakefront. East of Two Mile Lake. 1,800 square feet. $46,000 minimum.' " She looked at Saffron. "That sound cheap to you?"

"Cheap? Considering the condition, I wouldn't say cheap." Saffron retrieved a bottle of toner from the cabinet under the copier and filled the tank.

Mosey waved the fumes away and continued. " '525 Horse Meadow Road. Foreclosure. Lakefront. East of Little Saline Creek near Highway 27 Bridge. 1,900 square feet. $88,900.' "

"Now, that's a bargain." Saffron wiped her hands and went back to her chair.

" 'Arnold summer home. Estate sale. Lakefront. Little Saline Reservoir on McKenzie Lane. 1,725 square feet.' " She paused. "That's interesting."

"What?"

" '$50,000 or best offer.' I'd have thought that the Arnolds would've wanted more. It's been in the family forever."

Saffron shut down her computer and got up. "I'm out of here, missy. It's five o'clock." She swished around the edge of the desk and headed toward the coat rack. "Close up, would you?"

"Sure." Mosey looked up. "*Hasta luego.*"

"What'd you call me?"

"Rafael's going to teach me *castellano.*"

"Uh-huh, I'm sure he is."

Shopping bag, purse, and parasol in hand, Saffron stopped to shake a finger at Mosey. "You close up. Don't you forget, now."

"Hey, Saffron. You know anybody old?"

"Old? Like how old?"

"Ninety, a hundred."

"Big-Eye Brown, my great-great uncle." She leaned on her parasol.

"He live around here?"

"Sure does." She backed toward the door.

"I don't guess you'd want to ask him—"

Before she could finish her sentence, the door closed.

"Huh." She slipped into Saffron's chair and rolled backward toward the wall. She ran her fingers through her short, cropped hair again and again and, with each pass, pulled up the stubby remains of a once long "horse tail."

Bet you could flick some flies—

"*Mannaggia*, Daddy!" She could half see her

father's broad smile, prelude to a long, low chuckle. She pulled a folded paper from her straw tote and held it to the light. "Daddy, if you were here, I bet you could make heads or tails of this peculiar map."

But her daddy wasn't there, and her only close contact with the era of her father and father's father—who wasn't there, either—was Dot Cowsley. "Guess I could stop by Frye, Frye, and Humphrey and show this to Dot."

Better carry your crocheting with you.

"Daddy, she's not that long-winded."

Harrumph.

Chapter Five

By the time Saffron reached the nursing home where her great-great uncle Big-Eye lived, a nursing assistant had dressed the nonagenarian in his best suit of clothes and buckled him into a rocker on the wide veranda. The assistant had stuffed a clean, white pillow behind his head and shoved a sturdy foot stool under his slippered feet. In his day, T. Patrick Brown had stood as tall and strong as any man in Hembree, Eastside or Westside. But with the passing of time, his muscles had atrophied, his lanky frame had shrunk, and his dark brown skin, as smooth as a pecan shell, had folded into deep furrows. Yet time had shown T. Patrick some respect, sparing him his front teeth, upper and lower, a thick head of hair as soft and white as cotton, and a pair of eyes that radiated the raring-to-go attitude of the young T. Patrick. His eyes were no bigger than the next fellow's, but he'd been dubbed Big-Eye for his extraordinary fortune with the women of Eastside, the area where Hembree's African-American population clustered once the Union Army liberated the town.

"Uncle T.! My, don't you look fine!" Saffron said.

"Come on up here, young'un." He shifted in his chair, sending the wedged-in foot stool flying.

She rushed to his assistance just before he toppled onto the floor, rocking chair and all. "Who left you out here by yourself? I'm going to have to speak to these people, leaving you on the veranda by yourself." She pulled him into an upright position and righted the foot stool.

"Put me in a corner and I'm coming out!" he yelled, banging on the chair arms with his fists.

"Gotcha," she replied, giving him a gentle push that made him flop back in the rocker. "Now, you stay put."

"Stay put, huh."

"You had your supper yet?" She reached into her tote and pulled out a paper bag.

"I did. What's that?"

"You know what."

"Fried pies. Oo-we, I can smell 'em."

"What kind of fried pies?" She smiled broadly.

"Persimmon."

"Persimmon? And where do you think I'd get any persimmons?"

"Peach."

"Uh-huh, you want one?" She pulled out a crispy pie, placed it on a cloth napkin, and offered it to Big-Eye.

"Lordy, you're good to your old uncle. Yes, you are." He took a bite. "Uh, uh, uh. You cook better than your momma."

"Don't let her hear you say that." She leaned over and gave her uncle a peck on the cheek.

"She don't ever come see me."

"What you talkin' 'bout?" She pulled up a chair and sat down. "She's been here much as anybody."

"Huh."

"You want some water with that?" She handed him

a bottle of water from her tote. "They still feeding you good?"

He shook his head. "I ain't got no appetite."

"No appetite, except for fried pies."

He laughed. "Yeah, I ain't got no appetite, not like I used to." He took a swig of water and looked over her shoulder at nothing. "How's a body supposed to have an appetite, just sitting around staring at four walls?"

"We aren't feeling sorry for ourselves, are we?"

"You just wait."

"I know."

"You *don't* know, not yet. But you might know one of these days when you get old like me."

"Uncle Big-Eye, I'm not going to get old like you."

"You don't know that. All us Browns get old."

"You ninety or ninety-one?"

"I done lost count."

"You haven't. I know you haven't. You remember everything. I ask my momma something, and she says, 'Ask Uncle T. He's got the best memory of anybody around here.' That's what she says every time." She took the napkin from her uncle's hand and wiped his mouth. "That was good, wasn't it?"

"You got some more in that tote sack?"

"You know I do."

"Why don't you leave me one for later?"

"I'm going to leave you this whole bag. But don't you go eating them all at once."

"I won't."

She folded the napkin and slipped it in her tote. Then she took out a manila envelope and propped it against the footstool. "Tell me something, Uncle T."

"What's that?"

"You got your reading glasses?"

He pulled a pair of readers from the inside pocket of his sports jacket.

"Uncle T., you remember Mosey Frye, the lady I work with over at the real estate office? You know, the skinny blond lady that works for Mr. John Earle?"

"Yeah, I know who you mean."

"She's trying to hunt down an old house." She unfolded a copy of the map and handed it to her uncle.

"Huh."

"This guy comes into the office today with this funny old map. He wants Mosey to find a house for him. This one. See there by the pond?"

"Yeah, I see."

"Think way, way back, Uncle. T., to about the time of the flood, maybe some years after the flood, say, the late twenties."

"What is this place?" he said.

"Hembree. Think way back to the twenties, early thirties."

He looked up. "I was seven years old when the flood came." He shook a knotty finger in the air.

"That's right, I've heard you say that. Seven years old. All you Browns were living up at the Bilyeu place, and when the levee broke, everybody on the place had to crowd into the top floor of the main house."

"That's right. Nobody much had a two-story house back then."

"Not many people's got one now," she said.

"Fifteen people in one room, twenty maybe, all crowded together on the top floor, till the boats come for us. Um."

"Great-grandmomma was there, too, wasn't she?"

"Yeah, she was, and her daddy and momma and all the kids. We all stayed there, till the boats come."

"Uncle T., do you remember any Spanish man living in Hembree back then, right about that time?"

"Spanish man, um—I don't recollect. You say he come here after the flood?" He gave the back of his head a good scratching, then looked down at the map, running his finger from the round pond to the house and back to the pond. He cocked his head and looked up. "How come you asking me 'bout this?"

"Who am I going to ask, Uncle T.?"

"Ask your momma."

"Momma wasn't born yet."

"Huh."

"Think, Uncle T." She pulled the map toward her and pointed to one of the shotgun houses.

"All of us lived in shotgun houses back then, them's lucky enough to have a house."

"Did you live in one near a round pond?"

"Round pond...," he pondered, scratching his head again. "I don't recollect."

"Near the Civil War cemetery."

"We lived near the cemetery. I remember..."

"Remember what?"

"Them's was hard times, like you young'uns don't know nothing about. We had somethin' to eat 'cause we farmed, but nobody had no money. Nothin'. But then the union come 'round."

"What union?"

"The Black folks' union...sharecroppers."

"I know about that. But you weren't mixed up in it, were you?"

"Not me, I was too little. But my brothers, Eugene,

Thomas…"

"And that union man, that foreigner?" she said.

"Yep, sho' nuff was."

"You still remember his name?"

"I'm thinkin' him and Eugene were buddies. Hung out together over at—what was the name of that place? He had a guitar. He let Eugene play it. They wouldn't let me touch it. They played at the juke joint—what was it called? Eugene got some money playing at the juke joint with that fellow—what was his name?"

"Was it a Spanish name, like José, Juan, Pablo?"

"José. I think it was José, but Eugene called him—"

"Pepe?"

"Girl, you done read yo' Uncle T.'s mind. Pepe, that was it. Pepe."

"And this Pepe, he hang around here long?"

"I reckon he did. He got all mixed up in the strike. Yeah, all the cotton pickers went on strike, just as it got to be pickin' time. Momma, she say we didn't have no business getting in trouble with Mr. Jake. Momma say the whitecappers get us. Oh, Lordy, the whitecappers come 'round—"

"Did Uncle Eugene go on strike?"

"Sho' did."

"He get in trouble with the law?"

"Naw, Eugene was smart, smart enough to stay out of trouble. He knew all 'bout the whitecappers. He didn't wanna pick cotton no way. Said he was going to Memphis, play and sing at a juke joint."

"So what happened to Pepe?"

"He left town. Mr. Jake 'bout run him off."

"How come?"

"I don't know. Maybe Mr. Jake…"

"Yeah?"

The screen door opened, and the assistant stuck his head out. "Saffron, how you doing?"

"Fine, and yourself?"

"Can't complain. Mr. Brown, you ready for me to help you to bed?"

"Ain't time, is it?"

"Yes, sir. Time to get a bath, put on your pajamas. Let me help you in."

Saffron stood and passed the sack of fried pies to the assistant. "You keep these for Mr. Brown. He's had one, so don't let him go tricking you into giving him another one." She patted her great-great-uncle on the shoulder and watched as the assistant lifted him out of the rocker and into a wheelchair.

"Bye, darlin' girl. You come see your uncle any time you want, you hear?"

"Okay, Uncle T. I'll be back real soon."

Chapter Six

Mosey headed bright and early to McCutter & Sons to place John Earle's big order for business cards, desk calendars, stationery, and forms of one kind and another. Miss Evelyn McCutter, the owner of Hembree's office supply, welcomed her graciously at the door. Elderly yet chic, she wore an ironed-crisp, white linen blouse, navy-blue business skirt, and peep-toe, kitten-heel pumps. A tortoise shell barrette fastened back her silver-gray hair, parted and styled in a pageboy.

"How many of these notes does John Earle want?" Miss Evelyn's voice flowed out in a soft falsetto.

"It's not written down there?" Mosey said.

Miss Evelyn bent over her rolltop desk and moved her pencil down the list. "No, ma'am. Doesn't say how many."

"Doesn't say. Well, I guess a dozen plain notes and a dozen engraved, and do half with John Earle's initials, half with mine."

"That makes two dozen, half plain, half engraved."

"And if you don't mind, when the order comes in, deliver it to the office and send the bill— Well, you know where to send it. And by the way, those rollerball pens, the ones with the turquoise ink? Might as well include a box of those."

"Be glad to do that." She listed the last item and passed her clipboard to Mosey. "Just sign here, if you will."

Mosey signed and passed the clipboard back to Miss Evelyn, who began punching in the figures on an old-fashioned adding machine.

"Miss Evelyn, do you know anybody who's been around here, let's say, since the 1920s?"

"Let me think." Miss Evelyn stared vacantly into space. "There must be a few out at the Magnolia Nursing Home. I just heard a day or two ago Agnes Pruitt passed away. You know Miss Agnes? She taught at the high school for, gosh, fifty, sixty years." She went back to her adding.

"You don't mean it. I had her for eleventh grade math."

"So did I, and I'm twice as old as you."

"Miss Evelyn," Mosey said with a wink, "I wouldn't have guessed that."

"Ha!" After recording the sum on the invoice, she passed it to Mosey.

"You see, I have a copy of this old map." She pulled the pictograph from her tote. "One of my clients brought it in. Strangest map you ever saw." She handed it to Miss Evelyn.

"My word, I've never seen such a map, well, except maybe in a history book. This is Hembree?"

"It is. See there?" She pointed to the landmark she'd decided was the town square. "That must be the Square, and there's the courthouse and the Tavernette, don't you think?"

The octogenarian took off her aluminum-frame

glasses and squinted. "That could be the Tavernette. Uh-huh. But it's bigger than the courthouse."

"I know, but look at those chickens. They're as big as the pigs. And that pair of mules—did you ever see a mule with a braided mane and tail?"

"No, can't say I have. But I have seen pictures of mules just like that. In fact..." Miss Evelyn laid the map down and approached a bookcase filled top to bottom with atlases and manuals. She looked up and down the case, rubbing her chin. "Here it is," she said. "*Andalusia: Bullfights and Horse Fairs*." She opened the heavy, cloth-bound book and flipped to a group of photographs about halfway through. She balanced the book on one hand and tapped with her fingertips on a picture. Lean arms trembling, she passed the book to Mosey. "Look at that."

It was a picture of a team of eight mules, paired up and hitched to a buggy. They all had braided manes and tails, and every one was dapple gray.

"Uh-huh," Mosey said. "Now I see."

"See what?"

"Why the mules on the map look the way they do." She looked up at Miss Evelyn. "They aren't Hembree mules. They're Spanish mules."

"Spanish mules in Hembree?"

"Not in Hembree, but the cartographer sketched in a pair of Spanish mules."

"Well, they certainly look like Spanish mules, don't they? But why put—?"

"I'm not sure why he did it, but it's a pretty good explanation. The mapmaker was Spanish. He came here years and years ago, around the time of the '27 flood."

"The flood. My, my."

"According to his great-grandson, he did."

Miss Evelyn shook her head, as if to jostle the disparate facts into order. "And how did you happen to meet his great-grandson?"

"He stopped by the office yesterday. He was looking for this house." She pointed to the structure next to the round pond. "You don't happen to recognize this place, do you?"

"Not really." Her eyes wandered to the smaller house nearby. "This one looks like a shotgun house."

"Does, doesn't it?" Mosey said. "Hembree's full of shotguns, especially in Eastside. You know of one next to a round pond?"

"Round pond...that's the roundest pond I ever did see. Must be a man-made pond. And look at that boat. I declare. It's half the size of the pond. Huh."

"You can't depend on proportion, Miss Evelyn, not with this map. The cartographer obviously had a vivid imagination."

"Yes, I would say so." Her head bobbed gently. "And this relative of the Spanish cartographer, you say he's in Hembree?"

"That's right, and he's expecting me to locate this house."

"There's a roundish pond close to the old cemetery. A very small one. Man-made, I'm sure."

"That makes twice I've heard that place mentioned in two days. Guess I'd better drive out there and take a look around."

"Mosey, you need a *real* map of Hembree." She stepped over to a document file and, standing on tiptoe, reached into the top drawer and retrieved a stack of folded maps. "Take one of these. Over there in that old part of town there're a lot of little streets—lanes, you might say—that you may not know anything about."

Mosey accepted the map and fumbled in her tote for her billfold. "How much do I owe you?"

"Not a cent. I hand these out to visitors all the time. You take this map and compare it with that one. You'll figure it out."

"Thank you, Miss Evelyn."

"You're most welcome."

"Guess I'd better get on my way."

"Appreciate your business, Mosey, and tell John Earle not to be such a stranger."

"I'll tell him, but nobody sees John Earle except his golfing buddies, and I guess his wife sees him now and again."

With a wave good-bye, she left the office supply and headed in the direction of the newspaper, thinking she might drop off an ad. But deciding she'd better give the boss man a call, she pulled out her phone and called John Earle. "John Earle, hi. Mosey here. I placed that big order for you."

"Good. Thanks for taking care of that."

"You didn't say how many boxes of notes you wanted."

"Ten, fifteen."

"Well, it wasn't on the sheet Saffron gave me. I ordered twelve plain and twelve monogrammed, six with your initials, six with mine. You wanted pink, right?"

"Pink!"

She giggled. "No, I didn't order pink. Listen, I got a call from A. B. Bilyeu. You know him?"

"That old coot? I sure do."

"He's looking for a summer home on lakefront

property, and Saffron mentioned Larkspur. It's your listing."

"That's right."

"What about that couple from Ebenezer?"

"Waste of time. They said they wanted something move-in ready."

"What should I tell Bilyeu, then?"

"His nephew Cecil DeGroat was here yesterday checking out the place. He didn't stop by the office?"

"I don't believe so," Mosey said. "Saffron would've said something."

"Call him back and see what's up. See if he's willing to pay the asking price."

"How peculiar that his nephew was here," she said, "and didn't stop by."

"He was here on business, so he said."

"Okay, I'll take care of it. Talk to you later."

Mosey dropped the phone in her tote and looked around. Standing equidistant from McCutter and Sons, the *Gazette*, and her good friend Nadia Abboud's antique shop, she felt like a mouse in a maze. Which way to turn? Should she stop by to see Nadia, tell her about her new client and his old pictograph of Hembree? Nadia was the best antiquarian in town. She'd been in every historic house in the vicinity. And if the Bilyeu place had been the site of an estate sale, Nadia, for certain, would have attended. Or, would her time be better spent dropping the ad by the *Gazette*? She might bump into Tabbard Wilson. There wasn't an archive in Hembree he hadn't poked his snout in. But on the other hand, by walking a couple of blocks to the Square, she could press Dot Cowsley for information about Hembree in the twenties, maybe run into Carlotta. She never had gotten around to asking her about Waite House, though whatever her step-aunt might know about the Waites or Crumps seemed anticlimactic. That matter had been put to rest—or had it been? There was still that business about her daddy's admonitions: *Stay away from Waite House, Mosey—you hear?*

She'd left her truck—her granddaddy's old truck—just around the corner. A drive down Little Smith might be the best course of action. She could take a look at the Bilyeu place, better to inform A. B. of its suitability as a summer house. Might she run across the curious round pond on or near the premises? Was there such a pond in Hembree, or was it a figment of the Spanish mapmaker's imagination?

At the moment, Shepherd Realty was the last place on Mosey's mind. A real estate agency wasn't a bad place for an out-of-work songster *cum* psychologist to hang her hat temporarily. But, as time passed, her need to sell a house had been eclipsed by her yearning to do most anything other than sell a house. If, indeed, she had been a mouse in a maze, she might have sat up on her hind legs and peered gleefully at the way out that lay before her; for in a moment, the practical course of Mosey, real estate agent, had conveniently coincided with the more alluring itinerary of Mosey, amateur sleuth.

Chapter Seven

Wednesday, September 23, 10:30 a.m.
Larkspur Plantation

It was mid-morning still, but hot, hot as it ever gets in late September. As Mosey stepped into the cab of her truck, air flowed out, tinged with heat and the smell of old vinyl. She fanned it away and rolled the windows down. Then, pulling a bottle of water from her tote, she laid the maps—Miss Evelyn's and Rafael's—on the seat beside her. She cranked the engine and took off for the tumbledown estate that historians knew as Larkspur, Hembreeites, as the Bilyeu place.

It wasn't a very complicated route. She would take Little Smith toward Two-Mile Lake, past the Roadway Bait Shop and the Jeremiah Java Café. Somewhere along that lonely stretch of highway, she was bound to see it. She'd never been there but had a good idea where it was. As Rafael's pictograph indicated and Miss Evelyn's map corroborated, it lay northeast of Hembree proper near a part of town called Eastside.

The miles clipped by—five, by the odometer—and she assumed she was getting close. Must be, since she'd passed the familiar landmarks, but so far nothing like a plantation-style house had come into view. Saffron said a grove of tall cypresses stood between the house and the road. And, sure enough, there they were: the cypresses.

And there *it* was: John Earle's sign, tacked low on a cypress knee. She hit the brakes and skidded to a stop.

Then, turning off Little Smith, she followed a gravel lane through the Confederate cemetery and onto the estate. A lofty pair of magnolias, dotted with cup-shaped blossoms, stood at the entrance proper. A rickety fence, twined in wisteria well past flowering, stretched from the magnolias to the scant ruins of Larkspur's main house. She parked in front of the ruined mansion. "Wow," she muttered. Hadn't expected anything so old, so splendidly decadent, or…macabre. She stepped out.

Mosey, get back in the truck, would ya?

Ignoring her father's caution, she walked right up to what was left of the house. Ionic columns, peeling and sun-bleached, carried her eyes upward toward a hazy blue sky. The columns, three wooden steps, a dilapidated porch, a wide door, and the shutters and casings of floor-to-ceiling windows were all that was left of the façade. Not a single part of it served a purpose anymore. Yet, like some centuries-old folly on the grounds of a stately house, the remnants, detached as they were from a larger structure, had taken on a beauty of their own.

She climbed the steps and warily made her way to the entrance. With most of the front wall missing, the house offered an unimpeded view of the relics of the once lovely interior: a crumbling fireplace, the twisted metal arms of a chandelier, and floorboards of solid pine, scattered with shards of porcelain and glass. She stepped in and walked through the residue of the Bilyeu family belongings. Watching out for weak spots in the flooring, she spied what appeared to be a piece of flatware, picked it up, and, drawing a handkerchief from her pocket, wiped away the dirt. It was a silver sugar shell engraved with the letter "B." "What a lovely find," she said. "I'll take this to Nadia."

Despite her status as a real estate agent, she rarely thought in terms of development. Restoration, on the other hand, was a different matter. She wondered why no descendant of the owner, no local garden club, had come forward with a proposal for a grant? She imagined someone would eventually, but in the meantime, Nature itself had prettied up the crumbling mansion. A lacey vine with pink, trumpet-shaped flowers crept through the spaces between the floorboards and up the side of the chimney. A patch of shrubbery that had pushed through the hearth pulled a Sweet Autumn clematis in with it. The vine, twisting and turning among the branches of the shrub, at the partially intact mantel, burst into a show of white blossoms. She reached for a stem, thinking she might break off a piece, but didn't. It was too lovely just where it was.

She walked past the fireplace to the edge of the floor where the back wall had collapsed into the underbrush. A few yards away stood an eye-catching specimen, tall and triangular-shaped with drooping leaves and clusters of big, oblong berries. "A pawpaw!" she cried, then leapt from the floor to the ground. She pulled off a berry and pressed her thumbnails against the skin. It split in two, exposing rows of black seeds, nestled in golden custard. She pulled the halves apart and bit into the flesh. She picked a few more berries—as many as her tote would hold—and climbed back onto the floor. Sitting cross-legged, she finished the delicious fruit, leaving nothing but the seeds and peel.

She stood up, wiped her mouth and hands, and surveyed the landscape. A half-dozen pawpaws sprouted in the rich bottom soil along the river. Here and there, masses of rusty leaves peeped through the vegetation on either side of the house. In the split-log fence along the edge of the property, she recognized the wood of the same specimen whose fruit she had just sampled.

Pawpaw logs, of course, came the intrusive voice of her deceased father.

"I know all about these fences, Daddy."

I bet you do.

"You don't forget anything, do you?" She imagined her father's broad smile.

Why, darling, I wouldn't forget a thing like that. You nearly breaking your neck—or was it your leg?— jumping fences bareback. My God, your momma was fit to be tied. I can hear her yelling, "Mosey, I thought you had better sense." He broke off his droll harangue with a peal of laughter.

"Daddy!" she droned.

Girl, trouble is your middle name.

"Hmm" was her only retort. She had to wonder, though, if there was wisdom in what her father said. *Was* trouble her middle name? Should she know better than to roam around a secluded property on her own? For her, as her father well knew, the choice between *risk* and *boredom* had never been difficult. Or was it a choice even? No, it was more like a reflex to do precisely what a sensible girl would *never* do. So, on this occasion, as on countless others, she ignored her father's words, bounded off the porch, and made a path through the tall grass toward the true object of her errand. Not the crumbling main house—whose exploration she would leave for another jaunt—but the restored shotgun shack, the now-called *summer house*, which belonged to the

Hembree Bilyeus but had recently caught the attention of their Louisiana cousins.

The new house, situated not at the front of the lot where it ought to have been, sat midway between the cypress grove on the main road and a cotton field at the back. The field was picked, but enough bolls were left on the broken stalks to infuse the air with the smell of "Delta gold." The house, bigger than the average shotgun, stood in a clearing a hundred yards from the older dwelling. Some Bilyeu ancestor must have enlarged and renovated it, apparently, turned it into a home fit for a planter and his family. Why they had abandoned the main house, she couldn't be sure. There wasn't any sign of a fire, and if flooding had been the cause, the new residence was no better equipped than the older to withstand a significant rise from the nearby Mississippi River.

She came to the drive and continued on toward the house, where, from the looks of it, no one had lived for a good many years. As she drew near, she realized Saffron had been right. The place did look like *a pack of thieves had been living in it*. The grass hadn't been cut, the veranda swept, or the dust and cobwebs wiped from the porch swing and furniture. The window screens were torn and rusty, and the panes either broken or missing. She slipped her phone out of her pocket and made a list of repairs for John Earle.

As she rounded the house, she looked for damage to the walls and roof but found none. The structure, in fact, looked quite sound. But coming to the screened-in back porch, she stopped, spying something out of the corner of her eye. "Now that's strange," she mumbled. The wooden landing at the bottom of the steps had shifted to one side, leaving a gaping hole. She stared down and, in partial darkness, saw her own reflection. "Good grief, that's dangerous," she griped. "Why's it been left like that?"

She phoned John Earle but, getting a voice message, called the office. "Saffron, glad I caught you. I'm at the Bilyeu place; the summer house, actually. You were right. The screens are a mess, most of the windows are broken out. No wonder it's so cheap."

"I told you what it looked like, didn't I?"

"Uh-huh, I know what you said. Listen, you know if John Earle's been out here?"

"I doubt it."

"Yeah—figured as much. If you ask me, it ought to be condemned. There's a hole out here big enough to bury an elephant."

"A hole—where?"

"Right off the back porch."

"What?"

"Just what I said, a big hole. Might be a cistern—I don't know."

"It's not covered?" Saffron asked.

"Looks like somebody pushed the cover to one side."

"Call John Earle."

"I did. I got his voice mail. If you manage to track him down, tell him to get an inspector out here. And tell him if he's planning to rent the place, he'd better get Frank Ferguson or somebody out here immediately. It's got to be painted, the screens and windows replaced, and that's just for a start."

"Okay, I'll tell him." Saffron heaved a sigh. "You been inside?"

"Not yet," Mosey said. "I think I've seen enough for

today."

"By the way, A. B. Bilyeu called again."

"That's why I'm out here."

"Right," Saffron mocked.

"*Right*, yourself."

"You think you can fool me, missy? Sure as I'm sitting here, you're out there looking for that round pond on Rafael's map."

"Round pond?" She played the innocent. "I haven't seen any round pond."

A technical truth, for it was a half-minute later, after the phone call ended, that the noted landmark came into view, a hundred odd yards from the back stoop of the shotgun.

Chapter Eight

Wednesday, September 23, 8:15 a.m.
Morgue, Delta Infirmary

Chief of Detectives Gus Olivera knocked at the door of the examination room, and Dr. Eads McGinnis, wearing horn-rimmed glasses and a starched, over-sized lab coat, ushered him in. He took a look around, it being his first visit to the morgue since the coroner's arrival.

Housed in the hundred-year-old Delta Infirmary, the Hembree morgue revealed the Spanish Colonial tastes of an earlier generation. With a vaulted ceiling, terra cotta plaster walls, and flooring of geometrically patterned tiles, the long, rectangular space retained the obsolescent air of a sumptuous mansion.

"Looks the same," he muttered. A sniff followed. "Smells the same."

"What did you expect?" she said.

"Uh, nothing," he stammered. "Just thinking."

What he'd hoped but hadn't mentioned to McGinnis was that, at old Dr. McGinnis's retirement, the cavernous space might rise to twenty-first century standards. A remodel of the morgue might even prompt the addition of cutting-edge investigative procedures. He scanned the cracked plaster walls, the dimly lit surfaces, the antique furniture. Nothing front-line was likely to happen here.

"Where's Springer?" she said.

"He's getting things in order at the station." He hung his hat on the antique hall rack in the corner and, passing the coroner's dark wooden desk, thumped his knuckles against a stack of manila folders. "I'm expected back at nine."

"Let's get started, then." First, she offered him a handkerchief, then, picking up the sheet, revealed the dissected body of Ninon Bilyeu.

Holding the handkerchief over his nose, he squinted at the open abdominal cavity.

"This lesion," she said, "wasn't made by a switch blade or an ordinary kitchen knife. This is a wide, deep wound."

"I see that."

She gestured toward the exposed organs with a gloved hand. "Two centimeters wide and *quite deep*, serious damage to the internal organs—stomach, liver, pancreas—slight damage to a thoracic vertebra."

He stepped back from the body. "What are you suggesting, then—a hunting knife, what?"

"Could be a hunting knife. Definitely not a stiletto. Possibly a dagger."

His eyebrows shot up. "A dagger."

She nodded, then pulled back the sheet to reveal the entire body. "No abrasions to speak of, except for some slight bruising. She adjusted the victim's head and brushed back her hair to expose a bruise along the left cheekbone.

"She must have fallen in such a way—" he said, breaking off.

"Yes, the position of the body at the crime scene suggested as much." She lifted and turned the victim's right hand. "Some defensive wounds on the palms, but the extremities are clear. That's about it." She covered the body, then slipped off her gloves and tossed them in the trash. "As for foreign substances—"

"Any blood, other than the victim's?"

"No blood, no fluids."

"Hairs? Fibers?"

"Afraid not, Lieutenant."

"And her clothing wasn't torn?"

"There was a tear at the wound site, of course." She approached the instrument table and reached for two vials. "This," she began, her voice brightening, "is *Clostridium tetani*."

"*C. tetani*?"

"*Can* be found in the human body."

"Tetanus, yes, fairly common."

"But not in such quantities," she added.

"You're suggesting it was introduced by the blade?"

She nodded. "That'd be a reasonable hypothesis, I suppose, but then you'd have to wonder how bacteria contaminated the blade."

"A scuffle? Maybe it fell on the ground."

"I didn't see any sign of a struggle, did you?"

"Nope, no sign of a struggle." He rubbed his chin. But then, what sign *could* there have been in an open space. There wasn't anything to turn over or break. "The assailant, weapon in hand"—he clinched his right hand—"must have approached the victim, stabbed her, she fell backward…"

McGinnis, more interested in her evidence than his conjecture, apparently, held the second vial to the light of the dissection lamp. "And *this*." As she twisted it back and forth, fiery glints and a faint clinking sound came from the bottom of the vial.

He moved in close. "Is it an opal?"

"It certainly is."

"And you found it exactly where?"

"In the folds of her clothing, near the surface of the wound."

"It hadn't fallen off?"

"Blood sets fairly quickly," she said, "enough to hold a small gem in place."

"An opal." He hesitated, unsure what to ask next.

"I'm thinking something exotic," she said, "like a dagger with a jewel-encrusted hilt." She walked toward her desk.

"A dagger with a jewel-encrusted hilt," he repeated. "You wouldn't be putting me on, would you, Dr. McGinnis?" He tagged along behind her.

She glanced back. "Why do you say that?"

He shrugged. Why had he said it? He wasn't sure, except, of course, she had a way of disarming him. He scrunched his brows together and coughed.

She hunched over her computer screen, pulled up a display of antique daggers, and placed the cursor over an arrow-shaped blade. "The specifications of this one match the murder weapon exactly. The blade, near the hilt—see?—is a little more than two centimeters wide. The length is sufficient to produce the wound."

"So, a dagger, eh? Could be a dagger." He shifted his attention from the computer screen to McGinnis's workspace, cluttered with plastic bags containing items from the crime scene. Through the plastic, he could make out a small garden tool and Sister Clare's habit and shoes.

He turned the evidence of the case over in his mind: the victim, the physical evidence, and now the coroner's findings. "Tetanus," he mumbled, "inside the wound, made possibly by a jewel-encrusted dagger." He glanced at the slight woman at his side, imagined that her befuddlement must be similar to his own. Somehow she seemed to have glossed over it all. Determination stiff as her lab coat, ha! A half-smile crept across his face. "That's it?" he said.

"Pretty much." She pocketed her readers.

"Find any prints on the trowel?"

"Her own."

"No other bloody prints, then?"

"No such luck," she said.

"And the autopsy report?"

"Complete, signed, and dated. Would you like a hard copy, Lieutenant?"

"The online form is adequate, thanks."

Having gotten what he'd come for—indeed, a good bit more than he anticipated—he grabbed his hat off the hall stand. He arrived expecting a change in the place and was disappointed on that score, but the coroner herself seemed sharp, discerning. He was pleased.

Olivera returned to the police station and, opening the front door, found Springer slouched against the wall next to the water cooler. The witnesses to the aftermath of the murder were seated on wooden benches on either side of the entrance, except for Sonny Ferguson, who, standing, was popping his knuckles and looking around.

"Shall we go into the conference room, gentlemen?" Olivera gestured toward the door.

"You want coffee, Chief?" Springer said.

"Yes, and would you entertain Father Moody, take his prints, while I speak to the Fergusons?"

"Sure, Chief."

Moody, seeing himself separated from the others, addressed Olivera. "I thought—"

"This way, Father Moody," Springer cut in. "Let's get the preliminaries out of the way."

Olivera remained by the door while the Fergusons filed in. "I've come from the lab, where Dr. McGinnis has informed me that Sister Clare did, in fact, die from a stab wound to the abdomen."

"We aren't suspects, are we?" Frank Sr. took a seat and propped his elbows on the table.

"It's early in the investigation to rule out anyone."

"So we *are* suspects, then." He slumped back in his captain's chair.

"Look," Olivera began, "there's no need for alarm." He cleared his throat. "You've all had a night to think about this, so if you don't mind, please tell me anything, anything at all that might help with the investigation. The investigation, yes—let's keep focused on that, all right?" He pulled notecards and a pad and pencil out of his lapel pocket. "Let's begin with you." He looked into the oldest Ferguson's gray eyes. "How long did you know Sister Clare?"

"Like I told you yesterday, since she was a baby." Perspiration beaded across the elderly man's brow.

"You knew the family?"

"I knew her granddaddy Mr. Jake Bilyeu and her father Mr. Arnold and, uh, more recently, Mr. Emile. He managed the farm after Mr. Arnold passed."

The door opened and Springer arrived with a tray of steaming mugs. "Anything else, Chief?"

"Yes, actually." He wrote and, tearing the sheet from the pad, passed it to Springer, who read the message and left the room.

"And how, Frank, did you come to know the Bilyeu family?" He passed coffee to the seated men. "Sonny, would you care for some?"

The youngest Ferguson approached the table and picked up a mug.

"We sharecropped a hundred acres of their land," Frank Sr. replied. "We lived in one of Mr. Jake's houses till we moved to town."

"When was that?"

"After Frank Jr. was born." He paused to count on his fingers. "Must have been early seventies."

Olivera glanced down at his notes. "The deceased was born in 1955, and you were how old then?"

"I was born in '46."

"So you were about nine when she was born. Your contact was mainly with her father Arnold Bilyeu?"

"That's right. Mr. Arnold was the overseer then, but later on, after Mr. Jake passed, Mr. Arnold took over the farm."

"How well did you know Sister Clare?" Olivera's eyes remained fixed on the respondent.

"Pretty well, but she was a good bit younger than me."

Olivera referred to his notes. "She entered a convent at eighteen. You must have been…twenty-seven then."

"That sounds about right."

"You know anything about that, her entering a convent?"

Frank Sr. pushed away from the table and sat staring at the floor. "I don't, other than what was said."

"Go on." Olivera reached for a mug and a packet of sugar.

"She and her daddy didn't see eye-to-eye on certain

matters."

"Can you be more specific?"

"I don't really know. People said it had something to do with Mr. Jake." He lifted his head. "You know how it is around here, or maybe you don't. People like to talk."

Olivera made a notation before turning to Frank Jr., who had begun to tap on the side of his mug. "You have anything to add, Frank Jr.—about the Bilyeus? Sister Clare?"

The middle Ferguson bobbled his head. "I was just a kid when she left home."

"You weren't in school together?"

"I'd just started when she was finishin'. I remember she was a cheerleader."

"She was a popular girl?"

"And pretty as a picture," Frank Sr. interjected.

"Sonny." Olivera turned to the youngest Ferguson, who had taken a seat at the table and was popping his knuckles again.

"Will you cut that out?" Frank Jr. snapped.

Olivera glanced at Frank Jr., then Sonny. "Did you know Sister Clare?"

"I knew who she was." Sonny rubbed his cheek, where blond stubble was barely visible.

"You knew who she was." Olivera flipped to a new page. "But I guess you never talked to her, never went to the hermitage?"

"No, sir." He glanced away.

Olivera turned to the older Fergusons. "And what about you two—did either of you ever have an occasion to go inside the hermitage?"

Frank Sr. shuffled his feet. "No, don't believe I did."

"And you, Frank Jr.?"

He shook his head.

"Let's back up a second. When Sister Clare's father died, Emile Bilyeu took over the management of the farm."

"That's right," Frank Sr. confirmed. "Mr. Arnold worked it out before he died. His cousin would come to Hembree from New Orleans."

"Emile Bilyeu didn't live in Hembree?"

"Nope. I don't think he'd ever been here."

"And you continued sharecropping, as before, for Emile, I mean."

"That's right. Till later on, when Mr. Emile moved to Memphis."

"With Sister Clare gone," Olivera said, "who'll inherit Larkspur—do you know?"

Frank Sr. wrinkled his brow. "Couldn't tell you that, Lieutenant."

"Is there anything you want to add to your original statements, gentlemen?"

The three glanced at one another and shook their heads.

"Then, if you wouldn't mind signing." He handed each of them a typed document and pen. "And if you'll wait outside, Sergeant Springer will take your prints and a DNA sample."

After they left, Olivera cleared the table and looked out to see Father Moody pacing just outside the door.

"Sorry for the wait. Come in and have a seat."

Moody sat in the chair recently vacated by the youngest Ferguson.

"Would you care for something—coffee? I could ask Springer to bring a fresh cup."

"No, thank you, Lieutenant."

Olivera settled back in his chair and paused to study the face of the man who sat before him, hands crossed on the table. It was a pleasant face, unremarkable except for the eyes, as yellow-green and lustrous as a peridot. Perhaps men of the cloth, unlike children, are meant to be heard and not seen. He'd never noticed before—and perhaps one doesn't—that the priest was an attractive man, well-built for sixty. "Father Moody" —he scooted his chair in close and leaned forward—"I don't suppose you've remembered anything more, have you? You were upset, which, of course, is understandable. You knew Sister Clare better than anyone."

He lifted his eyes. "What was that, Lieutenant?"

"You knew Ninon Bilyeu, Sister Clare, fairly well, I would gather."

"You might assume that, but I'm not sure I knew her well at all."

"You were her confessor, were you not?"

"No, I was not."

"Do you mind if I ask who was?"

"Monsignor Mannix, at St. Patrick's in Conakry."

He jotted down the name. "Mannix, I should speak with him right away."

"Of course, if you think it would help."

"How long did you know the deceased?"

"Since she first came to the hermitage, some twenty years ago."

"Where did she live previous to her arrival?"

"She was at Perpetual Adoration, about seventy-five miles north of here."

"I see." He scribbled the name of the convent. "Do you know why she decided to seclude herself?"

"We never discussed it."

He paused. "You never discussed it."

Moody responded with a stare.

Olivera continued. "Did you see her regularly?"

"At mass. She was always at mass, of course."

"And did you see her yesterday?"

"Yes, briefly. I'd gone out for a walk and passed by the hermitage. She was in her garden, digging, I think it was. She stopped whatever it was she was doing to offer me a basket of tomatoes and peppers. Said she had more than she could eat. I accepted them and thanked her. She was an excellent gardener."

"What time was that?"

"Around ten, maybe a little later."

Olivera looked down at his notes. "So, you *did* see her after mass yesterday morning."

"Yes. Didn't I mention that?"

"According to your statement, Father—" He pushed a sheet of paper in the priest's direction. "—you only mentioned seeing her at mass yesterday morning."

Moody rubbed his brow. "Sorry, I guess I forgot."

"How often do you walk by the hermitage?"

"I take the path from the church to the hermitage and back, for exercise."

"And you, uh, often encountered Sister Clare?"

"No, not often. Occasionally."

"Pardon my ignorance, but do eremitic nuns, for the most part, stay inside the hermitage?"

"That depends."

"On what?"

"Well, the purpose of the seclusion, the inclinations of the individual—"

"And in Sister Clare's case?" Olivera asked.

"Sister Clare spent most of her day in contemplative introspection, I would think. Prayer, reading. She came to the sanctuary maybe once or twice a day—for mass, stations of the cross, prayer."

"And she had her garden, of course—"

"Yes, the garden. I suppose it took a good deal of time."

"And the parishioners—did she often speak to the parishioners?"

Moody shook his head. "I don't know, Lieutenant. What does it matter?"

Olivera cleared his throat. "Just one last question or maybe two, actually. Do you know if Sister Clare had any enemies?"

"Enemies? Oh, I can't imagine she did. She was not a worldly person."

"But, then, she was brutally murdered by *someone*."

"Yes, most brutally murdered." Emotion swelled in his voice.

"And I feel I must ask, given she was an heiress—we can't forget that, can we? Do you know, now that she's dead, who will inherit Larkspur Plantation?"

Moody heaved a sigh. "I have no idea, Lieutenant, no idea."

Chapter Nine

Wednesday, September 23 10:00 a.m.
Vieux Carré, New Orleans

It was mid-morning, and street cleaners were hosing water over the cobblestone streets of the Vieux Carré. Cecil DeGroat, carrying a suitcase, came out of the *porte cochère* of a hotel on Conti, turned south toward the river, and proceeded along Royal. At Napoleon House, he turned east and walked to the end of the second block. At a cast-iron gate, he set down the suitcase and rang the bell. Through an open window came the noisy banging of pots and pans—a ritual that preceded the preparation of meals at the Bilyeu abode—as if prior to peeling, chopping, and sautéing ingredients for a Creole repast, the clanging of iron on iron could empty the kitchen of malign spirits.

A. B. Bilyeu opened the gate. "Come on in. What took you so long?"

"I got here quick as I could."

"Never mind. You're here now. Lucille's making us a bite to eat." Bilyeu patted his belly, which bulged over the top of an alligator belt.

DeGroat set the suitcase on the damp tile floor and closed the gate behind him. He removed his straw hat and waved it in front of his face. "Damn hot."

"I'll turn on the air conditioning." Bilyeu passed

through the door and, looking back, offered to help him with his luggage.

"I can get it."

"You sure?"

He lifted the case and followed Bilyeu up a winding staircase to the living room. To his surprise, his uncle had updated the decor, replacing Persian rugs, Victorian loveseats, and marble-top end tables with light-colored carpeting, a chic black and white curved sectional, and a glass coffee table with a chrome base. White plantation shutters framed the tall windows, relieved at last of their heavily fringed brocade drapes. He looked around for something familiar. Only a few furnishings, portraits, metal sculptures, and myriad antique weapons remained as reminders of the Bilyeu Creole ancestry—their entrenchment, one could say, in the Crescent City's upper crust, despite the particular that gentility as such had never been their *métier*. An elegant gaming table, set with a posh *boîte de jeu* filled with French playing cards and stacks of porcelain chips, gave off a distinctive shimmer of France's Ancien Régime.

Bilyeu sat at one end of the sofa and reached for a cigarette from a silver box. "Care for a smoke?" He pushed the box toward DeGroat.

DeGroat sat across from him. "You know I don't smoke."

"Then you wouldn't want one of these." He snapped the box shut and picked up a cigarette lighter from the table. "Sure you won't change your mind? They're *designer*, as they say." He punctuated his boast with a decidedly nasal *hon-hon-hon*. "You may not get another chance," he chuckled.

DeGroat ignored the second offer but picked up the

lighter as soon as Bilyeu put it down. "This lighter—"

"Yes, that's the one."

"—it belonged to my father."

"He gave it to me. You want it?"

"I don't smoke." He put it down.

"I reckon that's why he gave it to me and not you." Bilyeu sent smoke rings toward an open window.

"I'd appreciate a little cool air, if you don't mind. It's hot as blazes." He loosened his tie.

Bilyeu stood. "It's getting on to lunch time. Care for something to drink? Lucille's made a pitcher of mojitos, if you're of a mind to drink before lunch."

"I'll take an iced tea, unsweet, if you have any."

Bilyeu left his cigarette perched on a cut-crystal ashtray and, exiting through the door to the kitchen, peeked back. "Care for something to nibble on?"

"No, thanks. Tea's fine."

He soon returned with a tray of frosty glasses and a plate of cheese straws. "Try one of these. Your momma used to make them. She gave Lucille her recipe." He set the tray on the table, then closed three windows and turned on the air conditioner. "Try one."

DeGroat picked up a napkin and a cheese straw.

"Lucille's a fine cook," Bilyeu said, "but your momma was the best cook in the family." He walked to the other side of the room and closed three more.

"Uncle Antoine, are you certain about all this?"

"What do you mean?" He sat and took a sip of his icy mojito, filled to the brim with fresh mint. "Lucille grows this mint herself."

"I did what you told me to do. I flew to Hembree and took a look at the house. It isn't fit for a dog, not as it is."

"Why, I know that, son. Nobody's lived there since your Uncle Emile packed up and moved to Memphis. But we'll take care of all that. We'll get it fixed up, painted. We'll get the garden restored."

"I took some pictures of the summer house and the old house, what's left of it." He pulled a cell phone from his pocket, opened the pictures, and handed the phone to his uncle.

Bilyeu scrolled through the pictures, then said, "Well, I didn't expect anything different, but, if you ask me, we've abandoned the place long enough. Time to put it back the way it was." He returned the phone. "We'll stock the pond, maybe build a pier. You'll see."

"So, you've told the agent—"

"Shepherd Realty?" Bilyeu shook his head. "They don't need to know, not right away."

"Because?"

"The family's been gone from Hembree for a long time, and our involvement, well…"

"Maybe you'd like to fill me in on exactly what our involvement *was* and in *what*." Less indolent than the Bilyeus, DeGroat was an attorney by profession and not a man to mince words.

"All in good time, son, all in good time."

As a DeGroat, however, he was more decorous than his maternal relatives—hence, his decision to avoid an affront to his aging uncle. Taking a sidestep away from the subject at hand, he got up and walked to a window. "You can just about see the river from here."

"You *can* see it from upstairs."

"By the way, when was it Uncle Emile moved to Memphis?"

"Yeah, I suppose you wouldn't remember that—you

and your sister were just kids. How is Emma, by the way?" Bilyeu stood and approached the window, mojito in hand. "She still in Savannah?"

"She is. She and her husband have done well for themselves. She's expecting a baby—did you know?"

"No, I didn't. Too bad your momma's not around to see that."

"Yeah, Momma loved kids. She'd have spoiled it to death."

"She would have"—he nodded—"just as she and I and Emile were spoiled by your grandmomma. Not a bad way to grow up. No, sir." He sipped to the bottom of the glass.

DeGroat repeated his question. "So, tell me, when was it Uncle Emile moved?"

"Let's see. He moved to Hembree around 1980, soon after Arnold died. He must have managed the farm a good ten years, maybe a little more."

"Nobody's been in the house since then?"

"I didn't exactly keep an eye on things up there. The land was leased to the man who owned the place adjacent to Larkspur. Darby? Dabney? I don't remember his name, but that fellow quit farming, and Emile wasn't ready to go looking for another tenant, being heavily involved in brokerage, or so he said." He chuckled.

DeGroat knew little of his dead Uncle Emile's business acumen, but, apparently, the idea of his running a brokerage firm was a laughing matter to his younger brother.

"Emile, that crazy fool." Bilyeu shook his head and, drawing a handkerchief from his pants pocket, wiped his face. "As far as I know, that somm'bitch just left the place sitting there."

"So, the summer house was empty all that time?"

"I couldn't guarantee that. Somebody could have lived in the house, uh, maybe somebody who worked for the man who leased the land. All I know is that Emile's dead now, rest his soul, and for whatever reason, he wanted you and me to manage the Hembree property."

"I saw Ninon…Sister Clare."

"Yeah?"

Then came a lull. Both men knew the resolution of the Larkspur matter entailed more than a business plan. A minute passed, and Bilyeu broke the silence with a condensed yet equivocal utterance. "There were things that were said and things that were *never* said."

DeGroat returned to his chair and glass of tea. "Yes, I know that. I'm afraid the time may soon come—"

The door to the kitchen sprang open, and the heady aroma of Creole food wafted in. Lucille Bilyeu emerged in a cloud of steam and, winking at her nephew by marriage, said, "Are you men ready for a little dish of crawfish étouffée? I've got bread puddin' for dessert." The red-faced, heavy-set woman disappeared as quickly as she'd come.

"I guess we're eating in the dining room." Bilyeu rose to go.

DeGroat remained in his seat.

"You coming?"

"What does she know about any of this?"

Bilyeu raised his index finger to his puckered lips. "Not a word."

Chapter Ten

Wednesday, September 23, 12:00 p.m.
Shepherd Realty

Shepherd Realty was a pleasant place, housed in a Colonial-style cottage shaded by cottonwoods and live oaks. The building itself was architecturally agreeable, and the surrounding lawn and shrubbery implied the attention of a constant gardener. Even at the end of a bone-dry summer, the rows of purple verbena that ran along the red brick sidewalk were as full and fresh as they'd been in May. Yet, as inviting a place as it was, Mosey sat stock-still in her truck, reluctant to get out and go in.

I know it wasn't *this* place—she thought, comparing the building before her with a house that had appeared to her in a dream. Though, alas, her knowledge of dream analysis was dwindling, her study of psychology had taught her that houses, more often than not, were symbolic of the self. The self...right. But sometimes— and Freud himself had said it—"A cigar is just a cigar." She smiled inwardly. So, maybe her dream house *was* just an ordinary house. She was a real estate agent, was she not? She got out of her truck and grudgingly advanced toward the entrance, pausing to pull up a volunteer peony from among the verbena blossoms. "It was my office, but it *wasn't* my office. Hmm."

In the past, she had occasionally dreamed about an actual house: a looming Victorian like Waite House or a secluded ruin like the Hansbrough mansion. Once, not so long ago, she'd dreamed about the House with a Corner Door, where the Westford sheriff found traces of blood from Rodger Billings's third victim. It was hard not to wonder if she had unwittingly specialized in stigmatized properties. Her dreams suggested that maybe she had. "That's it," she voiced. Therein lay her aversion to her office. She'd begun to fear houses, *all* houses, for the unseen forces they contained.

The sight of a familiar vehicle ended her ponderings. It was John Earle's sleek luxury car parked alongside Saffron's cool-looking muscle car. What in blazes had inspired that malingerer to show his face at the office? Her curiosity propelled her forward through the main door and into the reception area where John Earle sat chewing the fat with Saffron.

"Hey, Mosey." He slid off the stool he'd pulled up to Saffron's desk.

Making no attempt to syrup over her irritation, she picked up a stool and plunked it down next to his. "I've been wanting to talk to you."

A member of Hembree's idle rich, John Earle simply said, "What about?"—waiving the opportunity to excuse himself for his habitual absence from the office.

"The Bilyeu property. I've just come from there. It's pretty run-down."

"What'd I tell you?" was Saffron's shrill reproof.

Eyes narrowed, she glared at her co-worker before proceeding with her harangue. "And dangerous. There is a big hole under the back stoop deep enough to swallow an elephant, two elephants."

"You're exaggerating," he said.

"My point is if a person were to fall in—"

"The property is posted, Mosey." He looked at her fixedly, as if she were a headstrong kid. "I've already talked to Frank. He and Frank Jr. are heading out there this morning."

"Saffron can tell you. Not many places in Hembree qualify as summer houses. Mr. A. B. Bilyeu—"

"I suppose you haven't read the morning paper." He picked up the *Gazette* on Saffron's desk and opened it to the second page, where, from the pen of crime reporter Charles Tabbard Wilson, came a story describing the horrific stabbing of Sister Clare, née Ninon Bilyeu. "Sister Clare was found dead yesterday, stabbed. Frank Ferguson found her."

"Holy Mary, Mother of God!" Saffron crossed herself.

Mosey sighed and puffed out her cheeks. "For God's sake, who would kill a nun?"

"Emile, dead, and now Ninon, dead." His eyes lifted and rolled from side to side.

"Who's going to inherit Larkspur—is that what you're thinking?" Mosey asked.

"A. B. thinks they're in line for something."

"Do the police have any idea who killed her?" Saffron said.

"Looks like Olivera has called in the Fergusons and Melvin Moody."

"They aren't suspects, though. Surely not." Saffron stared at John Earle with questioning eyes.

"Well—"

Mosey interrupted. "So where does this leave *us*?"

"Us? Stuck, till they read the will."

"She'll leave it to the church," Saffron said.

"She probably did whatever her late father advised, unless—"

"Unless what?" Saffron leaned in.

"If it were my property—" He paused to refill his cup and sample a slice of warm butter roll. "I wish it *were* my property. Nice place for a high fence huntin' club."

"High fence huntin' club?" Saffron said. "What kind of big game you gonna hunt in Hembree?"

"Wild boar."

"Huh." She shook her head.

"The Bilyeus won't let go of it," he said, "not if they have a choice. When Emile left, he let Dabney cultivate the land, but he kept the buildings for himself. Every deer season, Emile was back here with his Memphis buddies, whooping it up at the overseer's house for a week at the time." His eyes settled on Mosey. "You saw what's happened to it. Might as well cart off the main house for kindling, but the overseer's house is salvageable."

"Salvageable, maybe, but I can't show it that way— it's not safe."

John Earle licked his fingers. "There's another angle to it. A. B.'s thinking about keeping the smaller house for himself, assuming the place stays in the family. Like I said, his nephew was just here. Flew up from New Orleans. So you see, Mosey, maybe we don't have to *show* the property." His eyebrows lifted.

"If Larkspur is titled in Ninon Bilyeu's name," she said, "an estate has to be opened and administered—"

"—prior to the property being distributed to the heirs," he concluded. "We do the paper work. Then, we collect the commission."

"So, why is the property listed? I went over there

expressly—" she stopped mid-sentence.

Don't lie to John Earle, Mosey. You know perfectly well—

"Hush, would you?"

"Come again," John Earle said.

"I went over there expressly to have a look around, for A. B. and Rafael."

"Rafael. Rafael who?"

"Rafael de Lobos, a young Spanish man. He showed up here with an old map—didn't he, Saffron?"

She nodded.

"Did he inquire about the Bilyeu place *specifically*?"

"Not specifically."

Halfway to the water fountain, he turned and said vehemently, as vehemently as a person of his languorous nature could, "Then show him another property, but hold off on the Bilyeu place till we hear something definite."

Stay away from Larkspur...

"Daddy!"

"Huh?" John Earle cocked his head.

"Nothing," Mosey said curtly, thinking her and her dead father's chitchats were none of his business.

"How's about some catfish salad, skinny lady?" Saffron said. "There's another serving over there."

"Skinny! Skinny yourself." Simultaneous laughter poured from three mouths. "I'm meeting Nadia at the Tavernette."

"Splitting a hamburger, I suppose." Saffron placed a thick slice of butter roll on a napkin. "Take this with you, in case you run into Rafael." She winked. "Tell him this is real Southern food—unlike that gentrified cookin' they slop up over at the Tavernette."

"Well, ain't you the persnickety one. I was going to

invite you to lunch, but never mind."

"I've already eaten, thank you."

"That serving of catfish salad? That was just an appetizer. Come on now. Get your tote, and let's go." Mosey slid off the stool, then looked at John Earle. "I don't guess you'd want to join the hen party, or would you?" If her ill-considered visit to Larkspur had nettled the boss, she was ready to make nice.

"No, ma'am, but I do appreciate the invitation. I've got some men folk waiting for me over at the ninth hole. You ladies go on, and have lunch on me." He pulled his wallet out and handed Saffron a fifty. "Will this cover it?"

"Half a burger each. I'm sure it will."

"Thanks, boss man," Mosey added.

"Saffron, you keep an eye on that one."

Saffron's glance slid from John Earle to Mosey and back. "You don't pay me enough."

"Hey!" Mosey exclaimed. She turned her back on her cackling coworkers and headed out the door.

Saffron and Mosey took off in Saffron's car and soon arrived at the Tavernette, which was packed as usual. They sat at the bar to wait for Nadia.

"I don't know why you like this place. Look at all that." Saffron cocked her head in the direction of a bust of Stonewall Jackson.

"Robert's working on it."

"How's that?"

"He's applied for a grant to move every bit of it to the Blanchard College Museum."

"Well, good for Robert. It's high time somebody did something."

Mosey waved at a passing waitress. "Miss, would

you bring us some iced tea, please. Unsweet with lemon for me."

"Sweet, for me," Saffron said.

"We're expecting a third party," Mosey said. "She ought to be here any minute."

"I'll be right back with those teas." The waitress dashed away.

"By the way," Saffron began, "my great-great uncle, T. Patrick Brown—"

"Yeah?" Mosey's interest piqued.

"I dropped by the Magnolia yesterday afternoon."

"And?"

"He knew Rafael's great-grandfather."

Mosey's eyes opened wide. "You don't mean it."

"I do mean it."

"Hey girl, John Earle been working you to death?" It was Nadia who'd arrived and, grabbing Saffron by the arm, wheeled her around. "Haven't seen you in forever."

Saffron stood and gave Nadia a hug. "You know it. Where you been keeping yourself?"

"At the shop, of course—where else?"

The waitress arrived with two iced teas. "I've got a table for you ladies if you don't mind sittin' in the game room."

Nadia glanced at her watch. "We'd better take it. I've got a customer coming at 1:00."

They followed the petite redhead through the bar and main dining room to the game room, where half the guests had abandoned their seats to watch a game of table soccer. Mosey, Saffron, and Nadia slid into a booth in the back corner, a good distance from the crowd.

"Miffy, table one," yelled the redhead, her eyes roving the room.

Her septuagenarian co-worker promptly waddled forth from the kitchen.

"Table one, Miffy," she said, pointing.

The older woman's gray eyes winced through coke-bottle lenses and came to rest, not on her customers but on a fly buzzing near Nadia's head. "How'd you get in here?" she admonished. Balancing glasses intended for another table on her tray, she swatted at the insect with her cloth, missing, before wiping the table clean. "I see Ruby took your drink order." She placed a menu in front of Nadia. "Miss, you don't want nothing to drink? Tea, lemonade—?"

"Bring me a lite draft, please, ma'am, and the house special, the roast beef with potato salad." Nadia handed her the menu.

"You want to split that?" Mosey said.

"Sure."

"And you, miss?" Miffy looked at Saffron.

"I've already eaten, so, tell you what—bring me a piece of lemon meringue pie."

The waitress's eyes fell on Mosey. "You don't want nothin'?"

"An extra plate, please, ma'am."

Miffy tucked her pad and pencil in her pocket. "I'll be right back with that beer." She waddled away.

"Look," Mosey said, waving. "That's Rafael."

The head of an energetic foosball player bobbed above the crowd. "Goal!" the player shouted.

The winning team cheered and slapped hands. The losers moved away, groaning and staggering, as if their defeat had occurred on real turf.

Saffron rose out of her seat. "That *is* Rafael."

"Who's Rafael?" Nadia said.

Winners and losers were congratulating the player who had scored the decisive goal.

Mosey stood and shouted, "Rafael, over here."

The proud player squinted and waved back.

"You won?" Mosey said.

"Yes, ma'am."

Mosey turned to her friend. "Nadia, this is Rafael de Lobos. Rafael, Nadia Abboud."

He clicked his heels and bowed slightly at the waist. "I am happy to meet you." His hazel eyes lingered on the pretty brunette.

"Won't you join us?"

"Oh, I don't think so. We have another game—best two out of three."

"You're a superstar *already*?"

"No, not superstar. That guy, he's the superstar. The one in the green cap, captain of the basketball team."

"Glad to see you're making friends," Mosey said.

"Can you tell me anything about the house?" he said.

"Not yet," she said, "but I *have* found a house near a round pond."

"Like the one on the map? May I see it?"

"I have to clear it with my boss first. It's his listing."

"Listing?"

"Yes, he was contacted by the family—"

"I see." His smile faded.

"We may be able to see it this afternoon, maybe, or tomorrow morning. I'll give you a call if I can arrange it, okay?"

"Yes, thank you. Nice to meet you, Ms. Abboud." He paused and looked at the woman who sat across from Mosey. "And to see you again, Ms.—"

"Smiley…Saffron Smiley."

"Yes, Ms. Smiley. Okay. I'd better get back to the game."

"Not so fast, Rafael," Saffron said. "I brought you something." She reached for the small parcel that Mosey had taken from her tote. "This is *real* Southern cooking. It's butter roll. I made it myself. Here…it's a pastry. You'll like it."

He opened the napkin and took a bite. "Delicious. Like…*palmera*."

"You like it?"

"Yes, thank you. Well, okay. See you later."

He backed away, nearly colliding with Miffy, who'd arrived with Nadia's beer and a tray of food.

"Pie for you, miss, and a house special for you ladies." She set the orders on the table. "And an extra plate."

"Could I get a refill?" Saffron held up her glass.

"You surely may. You want a refill, too, miss?" She reached for Mosey's glass. "Sweet or unsweet? I'll get you some more ice."

"Unsweet. And lemon, please."

With a "yes, ma'am," Miffy headed to the kitchen.

"Rafael who'd you say?" Nadia asked, returning to the subject at hand.

"De Lobos," Mosey said.

"Where's he from?"

"Spain."

"What's he doing here?"

"Looking for a house."

"You know what John Earle said." Saffron looked askance at Mosey.

"I know *exactly* what he said, but what John Earle

75

doesn't know won't hurt him." She pulled the pictograph from her purse and placed it in front of Nadia. "What do you make of *this*?"

"What's it of?"

"Hembree. Rafael's great-grandfather drew it from memory. He used to live here, long time ago."

Nadia examined the map, then glanced up at Mosey. "This must be the Square, and I guess this is the round pond you mentioned. There's a round pond at the Bilyeu place?"

"Sure is, and this must be the old overseer's house." Mosey tapped the house in question with a spoon.

"That *is*, in fact, the old overseer's house," Saffron chimed in, "and my grandparents used to live in it. As I was saying before, my great-great-uncle T. Patrick Brown knew Rafael's great-grandfather. His name was José de Lobos, but they called him Pepe, and he was here around the time of the Depression."

Mosey's eyes were glued, as were Nadia's. "Go on."

"As it turns out, Pepe worked for the sharecroppers union."

"Oh, my," Nadia responded pensively.

Mosey looked at Nadia, for whom the past stood toe to toe with the present. The mention of the sharecroppers union had carried her off somewhere. Mosey could tell. "So?" Her eyes slid from Nadia to Saffron.

Saffron put down her fork. "The labor riot—you know about the labor riot."

"Pepe de Lobos was mixed up in *that*?" Mosey said, as if she knew what *that* was.

"He sure was," she said, "as was Uncle T.'s brother, Eugene."

Nadia split the slice of roast beef and placed half on

Mosey's plate. "T. Patrick told you that? What else did he tell you?"

"Pepe and Mr. Jake were *not* on the best of terms. Pepe up and left. More likely, Mr. Jake ran him off."

"Jake Bilyeu?"

"The same," Saffron said.

Nadia fell silent.

Miffy arrived with a tray of refills. "Sweet for you, right? And unsweet with lemon for you?" She looked at Nadia. "What about you, miss? Can I get you another beer?"

"No, thanks." As soon as Miffy had moved away, Nadia continued. "What is Rafael looking for exactly?"

"Other than the house, he hasn't said." Mosey paused. "I guess it doesn't matter now." She held her plate out to Nadia. "Potato salad, please."

Nadia spooned a dollop next to the roast beef. "That enough?"

"Yes, thank you."

"Why doesn't it matter now?" Nadia asked Mosey.

"John Earle has forbidden me to go out there. It's not safe."

"Not safe?" Nadia said.

Mosey shook her head. "Besides that, the owner—at least we're assuming she's the owner—"

"Sister Clare, you mean," Nadia said. "I heard about that." She took a bite of potato salad and thought as she chewed. "Sort of interesting, isn't it? Rafael shows up—out of nowhere. Then, somebody stabs the owner of the house he's looking for."

Mosey set her fork down. "Rafael *didn't* murder Sister Clare, if that's what you're thinking."

"Sounds like a strange coincidence to me." Saffron

nodded her head slowly.

"He couldn't kill a fly," Mosey said.

"Who's to say? It occurs to me that Rafael is not as *naive* as he seems." Nadia shifted in her seat.

"What makes you say that?" Saffron sipped her tea.

Nadia shrugged. "I bet he's more attached to that house than he's letting on."

Mosey sighed and looked at Saffron. "She *knows* something—I knew she would."

"Hershel, the Bilyeu who initially purchased and farmed the land, was married to Fernanda de Lobos, an aristocratic lady of Spanish descent."

Mosey sat forward and raised her brow.

"When Arnold Bilyeu died," Nadia continued, "his only child, the now deceased Ninon—who had entered a convent by then—sold everything to the rafters to cover her father's debts. My father bought some nice pieces, including a large portrait of Fernanda de Lobos."

"Were you even born then?" Mosey picked up her glass.

"Yes, and I was very fond of that portrait. Daddy was, too. He over-priced it, to hold on to it as long as he could. Then one day, lo and behold, a man walked into the shop asking about pieces left from the Bilyeu estate sale. Years had passed but the painting was still there."

"It wasn't A. B. Bilyeu, was it?"

"I don't remember his name—maybe Daddy will. That same individual inquired about some family heirlooms that had gone missing when Fernanda and her husband left New Orleans. A pair of antique dueling pistols and a jewel-encrusted dagger."

"I guess you think Rafael came here looking for that stuff," Mosey said.

"Stuff!" Nadia exclaimed. "You have any idea how much that *stuff* is worth?"

"No, I don't, but I guess you *do*."

"No, not exactly, but you could ask Rafael if—"

"I don't see *me* asking him," Mosey cut in, "but *you* could. You could mention Fernanda's portrait, tell him you were wondering if he was related, the last names being the same."

"If Rafael *is* related to Fernanda," Nadia said, "then he's related to Sister Clare. He might be in line to inherit Larkspur."

"That's right," Saffron said, eyes open wide. "And if Rafael is kin to Fernanda, Pepe was, too. So what does *that* mean?"

"I don't know," Mosey said. "You think old Pepe had some kind of hidden agenda?"

"How could he *not*?" Nadia said.

"Huh?" Mosey wasn't quite following her friend's reasoning.

"Simple—too much of a coincidence," Nadia said. "Think. Pepe comes here to organize a union, and *it just so happens* that his Lobos relatives have settled here and own the largest plantation in the county?"

"Obvious, isn't it?" Mosey shrugged her shoulders. "So, you're saying he came *here* intentionally when he could have gone someplace else. Or maybe he didn't come here to do union work at all. Maybe he was after something."

Saffron glanced from Nadia to Mosey. "Pepe comes here, then Rafael—what *are* they after?"

Mosey looked at Saffron. "You reckon your uncle might have some idea?"

"I kind of doubt it."

"Hold on a second," Mosey said. "I've got a call. It's John Earle." She slid out of the booth and walked toward the entrance, out of range of the foosball players. "Hey, what's up?"

"Frank Sr. just called. Looks like they've spotted something in the cistern."

"John Earle, you sound worried. What'd they find?"

"Bones."

"Bones? You mean like human bones?"

"That's what Frank implied. The police are on their way."

"You called the police?"

"Yeah, Frank said it looked suspicious. I need you to get over there and take them the keys."

"Okay." She sighed. "I think I've got them with me. If I don't, we'll swing by the office."

"Sorry to interrupt your lunch."

"We're about finished. We'll leave right away."

She walked back to the booth and slid in next to Nadia. "Jesus, Mary, and Joseph."

"What's wrong?" Saffron said.

"The Fergusons are out at the Bilyeu place." She rummaged in her tote. "They found suspicious *remains* in the cistern. John Earle called the police. They're on their way out there, but they need the key to the house. He wants me to drive out and let them in."

"You got the key?" Saffron said.

"No, I must've left it at the office."

"You go on," Nadia offered. "I'll take care of the check."

Mosey and Saffron scooted away with a quick wave to Rafael, who didn't look up, deep into game two of foosball.

Chapter Eleven

Wednesday, September 23, 11:30 a.m.
Hembree Police Station

Lieutenant Olivera sat up straight in his high-back, faux-leather executive, his eyes fixed on the illuminated screen. Sergeant Springer strode in and placed a note on his desk calendar. He eyed it, then looked back at the screen.

"Carlotta Humphrey's number, Chief."

"And DeGroat's?"

"No luck. I mentioned it to Dot Cowsley. She knows everybody around here, and she hinted they had his info on file, but it was their policy—"

"—not to release their clients' telephone numbers." He heaved a sigh. "So, DeGroat's a client, too."

"She *did* say," Springer added with intention, "you might ask Ms. Humphrey." He backed toward the door. "Anything else, Chief?"

Olivera picked up his empty cup and handed it to Springer, who accepted it but didn't leave. He set it down on the desk and stood digging banana chips from the bottom of a plastic bag.

"What?" Olivera said.

"Frank Sr. called."

"What'd he want?"

"Says there might be some new evidence."

He pushed back from his desk. "New evidence?"

"There's an old cistern—"

"Cistern?" He sighed again. "If it wasn't at the crime scene— Oh, never mind. Bring the coffee, would you? I have a murder investigation to organize."

Springer picked up the cup and left.

"Persons of interest," Olivera muttered. He had the Fergusons at the top of the list. Which made sense. They discovered the body. On the other hand, how could they have left the thicket, committed the crime, returned to the thicket, then gone back to the hermitage without leaving tracks or being seen? "Highly unlikely," he muttered. And besides that, what motive did they have? He clicked on McGinnis's crime scene report and read aloud, as if better to commit the witnesses' movements to memory. "Blood-stained tracks leading from the victim's body to the truck matched the shoe prints of Frank Ferguson Sr., who, subsequent to kneeling next to the body..." He stopped and scrolled to the next page. "A second set of tracks, matching the shoe prints of Reverend Melvin Moody..." He looked back at the witnesses' statements. They were in sync with McGinnis's findings. He pushed back from his desk, clasped the back of his neck with his hands, and slowly rolled his head. He did that for a minute or two, then scooted back toward his computer. He'd been at it for an hour, and though he hadn't come up with any answers, he was beginning to extract an *idea of the crime*, which to him was essential.

He reached for an index card with his *map*—as he called it—of the crime scene. With a red marker, he drew a dotted line between the body and the elder Ferguson's truck, then, between the truck and the path to the church. He put down the red marker, picked up a blue one, and dotted again, this time between the body and the benches at the entrance to the hermitage. Setting both markers aside, he brought his eyes to rest on the small bronze box that held his writing instruments—a pyx it was called. Nick Ramos, his partner at the Santa Clara department, had given it to him as a memento of their last jaunt around the historic district. He emptied the contents into the top drawer of his desk, then held the pyx at eye-level. The original St. Clare, patron saint of Santa Clara, California, had chased off a bevy of Sicilian soldiers with an object much like the one he held in his hand—a replica of the sacred pyx used to transport *la hostia*, the consecrated host.

His thoughts slipped back to that last ramble with Nick. They had stopped at the mission gift shop, and, as they were leaving, Nick had handed him the pyx and said, "Olivera, *que la Santa esté contigo doquiera que vayas.*" He wasn't a religious man. Neither was Nick. Nor did they speak to each other in Spanish as a rule. Why, then, had he chosen those particular words, *que la Santa esté contigo...?* May the Saint be with you wherever you go. He set the pyx down and propped the index card against it.

Another day in mid-June, a few weeks before he'd left Santa Clara, he sat at his desk at the station, *mapping*, as now. On that occasion, his *map* plotted the movements of Father James Galloway, a suspect in a double homicide. A homeless person had found the bodies of two members of the altar guild in a dumpster near the rectory, and Galloway was at the top of the suspects list. His interview with the priest hadn't gone well. He'd sensed a vague hostility in the man. But his super yielded to pressure from the clergy and ordered him to remove

Galloway's photograph from the evidence board. He dug in his heels, refused to take it down, and, soon after, his dismissal arrived. Though he preferred to believe he'd preempted Wright's decision and resigned, he had not. Before he'd had a chance to fill out the papers, the letter appeared on his desk, clearly stating the reason for his termination. *Insubordination.* He ripped it up right in front of him, shouting, *Clericalism, this rotten system of protection and secrecy...*

He rose abruptly from his seat and angled himself toward the doorway. "Springer, coffee!" He sank back in his chair and took a breath. "Let it go, Gus," he said, echoing his partner's advice. He might have been able to let it go, if the evidence in the case hadn't proliferated and, in due course, outweighed the so-called *facts* of the case. Huh. Wright had kept telling him to stick to the *physical evidence*, but he was certain there was more out there. His take on the case had not been in error, and if Wright hadn't fired him, he'd have closed it. He shook his head, took another deep breath.

Because of his so-called insubordination, he'd lost his job. But to his credit, he hadn't let it get him down. He'd moved on, found another job. And, even more challenging, he'd adjusted to the colossal step-down from Santa Clara Chief of Detectives to Hembree Chief of Police. He propped his elbows on the desk and stared at the screen, his eyes moving back and forth between the coroner's report and the suspect list. He adjusted, yes, except at times such as these when he would have given his right arm for a touch-sensitive digital display, a bona fide investigative team, and, first and foremost, a partner like Nick Ramos. Springer and Reagan, good men that they were, lacked the training needed for top-notch investigative work. Eads McGinnis, on the other hand, was well-trained, intelligent, clever, but brand-new at the job. Easily as clever, if not as experienced, as.... What was his name? A year had passed, and he was beginning to forget things, like the name of the forensics specialist who wrote the autopsy reports on the double homicide.

He exhaled loudly and focused again on the case at hand. He perused the list of suspects. "Hard to call them suspects," he mumbled. People of interest, yes, but suspects? About mid-list, he came to the name DeGroat and muttered, "a complete unknown." He glanced at the note Springer had placed on his desk calendar. Maybe he should take a break, drop in on Carlotta Humphrey, see what she knew about the victim's will and, in passing, mention DeGroat. She might know something. It was worth a try.

Springer came in with a mug. "Here you go, Chief."

"Thanks, Springer." He stretched back. "Did you get a number for Mannix?"

"He wasn't on the list, was he?"

"Well, put him on the list. And call Frye, Frye, and Humphrey again. Tell Dot I'll drop by this afternoon— if Ms. Humphrey can spare the time. Tell her it's about the will, Ninon Bilyeu's will." He paused. "No, tell her I need to speak to Ms. Humphrey on a matter related to the Bilyeu homicide."

He wanted to see the will. He needed information on DeGroat. What else? He eyed the pyx again, mumbled something under his breath.

"What's that, Chief?"

"Nothing, just make the call, please."

"Fine, Chief, right away."

He let his hands drop to his sides. "Father Moody,"

he said as he tapped the side of the chair. Should he allow for the possibility...? Thinking back to the interview, he wondered why he hadn't asked the obvious question. Why wasn't *he* Ninon's confessor?

His thoughts wandered again to the Santa Clara homicides, and he recalled Galloway's admission to having heard the confessions of both victims within a week of the discovery of the bodies. He knew something about those women but wouldn't say. Couldn't get him to say.

Catching sight of the empty pencil holder, he gazed at the engraving of Santa Clara. She, too, like Ninon, had rejected comfort and privilege for poverty and seclusion. Neither her family nor the Church hierarchy approved, but St. Francis came to her aid, provided a modest place of seclusion for her and her small community of nuns. *¡Cielos!* Why hadn't *somebody* been around to protect Ninon Bilyeu? He leaned back and let his eyes roam the room. But why would this nun need protection? Was there some unpleasant family business he didn't know about? Some Church matter? Some...? "If I knew that," he said aloud, "I might have a vague idea of a motive." He set the pyx back in its place and stuffed it with pencils and markers.

Springer popped his head in. "You say something?"

"Nothing, nothing important. Did you speak to Dot Cowsley?"

"Dot says Carlotta is free around four, if you want to stop by." Springer's cell phone buzzed in his back pocket. "Hold on, Chief." He pulled out his phone and walked to a spot of semi-privacy on the other side of the partition. "Springer here." ... "That's right." ... "I see. He called here earlier." ... "Right, about the cistern." ...

"What's the problem?" … "Remains, *human* remains."
… "You say he's pretty sure they're human remains." …
"The Bilyeu place, near the old overseer's house." … "I
see." … "Certainly. Right away."

Guessing at the inaudible parts of the conversation,
Olivera slipped on his sports jacket, grabbed his hat off
the rack, and checked his pocket for his keys. "Let's get
going, Springer. Reagan can bring us whatever we need
in the way of equipment." He crossed the outer office,
and Springer followed, scooting out the door behind him.

"John Earle says the cistern is a good ten feet deep,
maybe fifteen. How we gonna get 'em outa there?"

"I'm sure Frank Sr. will have some idea about that.
You drive, Springer." He sat on the passenger side and
waited for Springer to take the wheel. "Where exactly is
the cistern?"

"Off the back porch of a shotgun house over at the
Bilyeu place." Springer cranked the engine. "It's about
five miles from here."

"Does Frank have the key to the place?"

"I guess not. Somebody from the real estate office is
gonna meet us there."

They took Main Street out to Little Smith, and as
Springer turned onto the road, Olivera glanced back at
the police station as it blurred, then disappeared. Hard to
imagine a less pretentious place, but appearances didn't
matter. Not to him. What really mattered was autonomy,
and that he had in spades. Yep. That he had.

Chapter Twelve

From the passenger seat, Mosey sensed Saffron's growing apprehension. Along the lane that led through the cemetery and past the magnolias, Saffron tapped, tapped, tapped against the steering wheel with the back of her graduation ring.

"You okay?" She glanced across at Saffron, who nodded, though her knitted brow suggested otherwise.

At the end of the drive, Saffron pulled up to a picket fence and stopped. "Looks like we're the first ones here." She opened the door and stepped out.

"Yeah, wonder what's keeping the lieutenant?" She stepped out and, shielding her eyes from the broiling sun, looked up at a cloudless sky. There was no white or blue, just a glistening haze that incubated the earth in moisture and heat. A short distance away stood the overseer's house, which she'd come to think of lately as the summer house. To Mosey Frye, real estate agent, it was a run-down house with peeling paint—a three-room shotgun converted into a cottage of the North Shore style. To Mosey Frye, amateur sleuth, however, the listing was turning into a great deal more. She wasn't sure yet what, but chances were, two of her clients, A. B. Bilyeu and Rafael de Lobos, were *people of interest* in Gus Olivera's investigation. No one had said it, but it was easy enough to figure. "We can leave the door open for Olivera and get out of here, if you want," she said to Saffron.

"I haven't been here in a long time—that's all."

Frank Sr. and Frank Jr., who had made themselves comfortable on the veranda, stood as they approached.

"You guys know Saffron, don't you?" Mosey said.

Frank Sr. took off his hat. "Howdy do, ma'am. We've met before, I'm thinkin'."

Saffron gave a half-smile. "How you do?"

"We brought the key," Mosey said, "just in case somebody needs to get in."

"John Earle told us to take a look at the cistern," Frank said, "but we've, uh, been looking around the outside, too. It could use a coat of paint, and, uh, some of the screens and windowpanes need fixin'."

"Yeah, it's not fit to show the way it is." Mosey took a step toward Frank Sr. "John Earle said you found something in the cistern."

"We sure did."

"What?—if you don't mind my asking."

"We lifted the platform," Frank Jr. pushed in, "and I was about to go down in there to check for leaks—"

"He started hollerin' like crazy," Frank Sr. said. "Like-to scare me to death."

The sound of tires grinding against gravel brought the Fergusons' story to a halt. Olivera and Springer drove up to the fence. Eads McGinnis followed close behind. They got out, unloaded the usual paraphernalia, then came toward the house, Eads with her leather bag and camera, Springer with cones and crime scene tape.

Olivera eyed the Fergusons. "Anybody been near the cistern other than you two?"

"I was out here day before yesterday," Mosey said, "and happened to—"

"Ms. Frye," Olivera cut in. He tipped his hat to Mosey and Saffron.

"Lieutenant, this is Saffron Smiley, John Earle's personal assistant."

"Nice to meet you. I guess you ladies brought the key to the house?"

"We did," Mosey said.

"We'll be starting with the area around the cistern but, Ms. Frye, if you wouldn't mind opening the door."

"Sure, Lieutenant." She dangled the key toward Saffron. "Do you mind…?"

Saffron nodded and, key in hand, walked toward the front. Mosey stayed behind.

Springer put on protective footwear and taped off an area around the cistern. Once the last cone was in place, he stood staring into the hole, then, turning to Olivera, said, "Chief, it's gonna take a backhoe, I bet."

"I don't know about that," Olivera said.

Frank Jr., plenty eager to help, apparently, said, "Me and Daddy got all the equipment you need, Lieutenant."

"But, if you don't mind me saying so—" Frank Sr. intervened.

"What's that, Frank?"

"The walls might be a little shaky." He wiggled his hands. "If they wuz solid, this here hole 'ud be full of water. There's got to be a leak somewhere."

"The downspouts are connected," Frank Jr. said. "Could be the pipe's sprung a leak. We could get it back up-and-running."

"So, what do you suggest?" Olivera said.

"I 'spect Frank Jr. could climb down in there with a

rope ladder, but problem is the walls might give way." He frowned and scratched the top of his balding head.

Olivera glanced at Eads, who had been speaking into a digital recorder. "Any experience with this sort of thing?"

She clicked off the recorder. "Not really."

"Lieutenant." Mosey moved closer to the group.

Olivera raised an eye.

"You might contact the Anthropology Department at Blanchard."

"Yes, how could I forget?" he said, sarcasm scarcely veiled. "The Hansbrough case…"

"That's right. Robert and Hugh—I'm sure they'd be glad to help."

"Well, if they wouldn't mind giving us a hand."

She reached in her tote for her phone, called Robert, and, within the half-hour, he and Hugh pulled up in Hugh's '49 ragtop.

"Ellison…Jessup," Olivera said. "I guess she filled you in." He aimed a thumb in Mosey's direction.

"You've got some remains at the bottom of a cistern, so we hear," Robert said.

"That's right." Olivera nodded.

"We need permission from the owner to excavate?" Jessup said.

"Yes, the legalities." He paused, rubbing the back of his neck. "I've got to speak to Carlotta Humphrey this afternoon. I'll ask her about that. But since we're looking at this as a crime scene…"

"In that case," Robert said, "it shouldn't hurt if we get started on the groundwork."

"I don't see a problem with that." Olivera shrugged. "What will it involve?"

"We'll have to shore up the walls with planks to avoid a cave in." Robert stooped and looked into the hole. "And once that's done, it's a matter of climbing down a rope ladder with a few implements." He walked to the opposite rim of the cistern and peered down.

"You think you could take care of this in a timely fashion?" Olivera looked first at Robert, then Hugh. "Given the situation…"

"I could start today," Robert said. "That work for you, Jessup?"

Hugh glanced at his watch. "I've got class in less than an hour, but if you could get the boards in place, we could meet back, say, around three-thirty?"

Once Robert and Hugh had left, Mosey said to Olivera, "Lieutenant." He didn't look up, and she said it again, a little louder. "Lieutenant Olivera."

"What's that?"

"If you don't mind my asking," and, of course, she imagined he did but continued anyway, "uh, you think there might be a connection between Sister Clare's death and these remains?"

"I wouldn't want to speculate."

"You know her family owned—"

"Like I said, I wouldn't want to speculate."

"Sorry, I was just thinking." She took a deep breath and relaxed. He was not going to get a rise out of her— it was too dang hot. "But never mind," she continued, "I'm sure you'll figure it out," she dropped her voice, "sooner or later."

"You'll *excuse* me." His eyes widened. "But I need to finish examining the crime scene. So, if you'd move back away from the yellow tape."

"Sure, Lieutenant, whatever you say." She retreated

to the veranda steps and took a seat next to Saffron, who was talking on the phone. "Problem?" she mouthed.

Saffron shook her head and mouthed back, "John Earle." She ended the conversation and slipped her phone into her pocket.

Mosey swatted a mosquito. "What'd he want?"

"Just making sure we got here." Saffron walked to the edge of the veranda, from where she could see the cistern. "How long you reckon that body's been down there?"

"No idea." Mosey swatted another. "But I imagine whoever performs the autopsy will figure it out."

"You don't suppose it was down there when my family was living here?" She came back to the steps and sat next to Mosey.

Mosey eyed Saffron. Damp with perspiration, she looked quite dry around the mouth. "Saffron, you okay?"

"Umm—not really."

"You aren't going to be sick, are you?" She pulled out a handkerchief and offered it. "You want some water?"

"I've got a bottle in here somewhere." She rambled in her tote, found her bottle, and took a sip.

"Well," Mosey said, "I hate to say it, but bones don't end up in a cistern when a person dies a natural death. You, uh, thinking you might've known, or maybe somebody in your family knew him or her?"

"It wasn't a Bilyeu—we know that," Saffron said. "All the Bilyeus are accounted for, aren't they?"

"Well, I'm not sure," Mosey replied—as if Saffron's "aren't they" had been an actual question and not a rebuke. "Why? You think it was a sharecropper?"

"I don't know."

"If it *was* a sharecropper, reckon what happened to him."

She opened her mouth as if to speak but then shut it.

"Surely not…" Mosey's words trailed off. Suddenly she felt a chill, as if a rabbit had run over her grave.

Saffron took a sip of water and scanned the dry, cracked ground around the veranda. "When I was just a little girl, I used to sit here on the steps with Uncle T. Patrick. I'd say, 'Uncle T., what if the ground just keeps on cracking?' And he'd say, 'Silly girl, the rain'll come and fill up all the cracks.' And I'd say, 'But what if I fall in, Uncle T.?' And he'd say, 'Uncle T.'d pull you out by your pigtails.' Then he'd lunge forward with his long arms stretched out, and I'd squeal and run down the steps."

"You guys are close, aren't you?"

"Yeah, Momma stayed pretty busy, but Uncle T. was too old to work much. During the day, he mostly hung out on the porch."

"You know of anybody who went missing?"

"Not while we were living here. But I do remember hearing about Uncle T.'s brother Eugene. He up and left, didn't tell anybody he was leaving."

"Why'd he do that?"

"I don't know."

"Did he ever come back?"

"I don't think so. They went looking for him but couldn't find him. Figured he went to Memphis. He said he was going to get a job playing at a night club."

"He never wrote, never called?"

"Not as far as I know." She took another sip of water and set the bottle on the step.

"But surely he would have kept in touch with his

family. He didn't leave on bad terms, did he?"

Saffron shrugged. "People didn't say much about Uncle Eugene."

Apparently, not. And all of that—whatever *all of that* was, and even Saffron didn't seem to know—had happened around the time of the flood and that *other business* that Nadia had spoken about. If Eugene had been involved with Pepe and the sharecroppers union...

Saffron tapped her on the shoulder.

"What?"

"Uncle T. said his momma warned Eugene against getting mixed up in the sharecroppers union."

"Oh, yeah?"

"Mr. Jake and the strikers were natural enemies."

"And Jake Bilyeu was the owner back then?"

"I think that's right. Arnold was running the place by the time we came here."

Mosey stretched her arms out in front of her, then stood up and stretched her back. "We're getting ahead of ourselves. We don't know how long that skeleton has been down there or even if it's a man or a woman."

"I know, I know."

Olivera rounded the corner of the house, followed by Eads. As they approached the steps, Mosey stepped to one side. "You ready to take a look inside?"

"We appreciate your opening up for us," he said.

"We could wait," Mosey offered.

Saffron reached in her tote for the keys. "Or, if you want, we could pick up the key at the station later on, whenever you finish."

"There's no need for you and Ms. Frye to wait."

Mosey looked at Olivera. "So, this entire area is a crime scene now?"

"That's right."

"I won't be able to show the house?" She asked that, though John Earle had already made it perfectly clear she wouldn't be showing it anytime soon.

"Afraid not," he said.

"Okay, then." Saffron handed him the key.

"Guess we'll go ahead and go," Mosey said.

"Just leave the key in the door," Saffron said, "and let us know when you're through."

He took the key, tipped his hat, and continued up the steps.

She and Saffron headed to the car. Mosey looked back as Olivera pushed the door open, held it back for Eads. "That guy's learning some manners, at least where Eads is concerned."

"Huh, he's got a little crush on the coroner."

"I bet he does."

Chapter Thirteen

Wednesday, September 23, 4:00 p.m.
Frye, Frye, and Humphrey, Attorneys

Olivera knocked, received no answer, and hesitantly opened the door to the outer office of Frye, Frye, and Humphrey. It was a spacious room, softly lighted, with portraits covering the wall behind the reception desk. A pair of upholstered wing chairs stood against a wall of bookshelves with leather-bound volumes. Certificates that attested to the partners' professional prowess, he imagined, hung above a brown leather sofa. He took a seat and leaned against a buttery soft cushion. Exactly the sort of place a person could get comfortable.

A quarter of an hour passed. So far, no one had come to invite him—*if he would please*—to enter the office of Carlotta Humphrey. He'd been told she would be free by four. Something must have come up. He lifted one leg onto the sofa, not daring to lift both, and nestled his head against the pillow. Just as he sunk into a state of vague mindfulness, the door to the stairwell opened and in came Dot Cowsley.

"Lieutenant Olivera, I'm sorry. Has Carlotta kept you waiting?" She shook her head. "Tsk-tsk-tsk."

He sat up, both feet planted, to face the short, plump septuagenarian, secretary to a line of Fryes, no doubt, and now to Carlotta Humphrey, Amos's step-daughter.

The essence of charm apropos the *face* of Frye, Frye, and Humphrey, Dot padded to her desk, unimpeded by high-heel pumps. She checked her phone for messages, then approached. "What can I get you, Lieutenant? A glass of iced tea, or maybe you'd prefer a cup of coffee?"

"Coffee, if it's not too much trouble."

As she passed the coffee table, she paused to straighten the magazines. "I'll be right back. Cream and sugar?"

"Sugar, no cream, thanks."

Another quarter hour ticked by, during which he drank his coffee and chatted with Dot. At four-thirty, the door opened again, and in came Carlotta. She wore a pale pink linen sheath, rumpled from bodice to hem, and sported a pair of hand-tooled western boots, as if she'd come from the fairgrounds instead of a board meeting at the Chamber of Commerce. "So sorry, Lieutenant," she began. She tugged at the clamp at the nape of her neck, unleashing a flurry of brunette curls. "These meetings go on and on—you know how it is. Got away as soon as I could."

He backed away from the bookcase to which he had wandered and smiled at Carlotta. "Ms. Cowsley has been keeping me company."

Dot handed Carlotta a stack of papers and accepted her briefcase in return.

"Bring us the Bilyeu file, please, ma'am, and that'll be all for today."

"Maybe Lieutenant Olivera would care for a refill?"

"No, ma'am, I'm fine."

"Well, I'll be going, then," Dot said. "Carlotta, that top slip—"

"Yes, I see." She checked the message to which Dot

referred. "I'll call him before I leave."

Olivera followed Carlotta through the door and took a seat in one of the upholstered chairs. Dot popped in with the requested file, which she set on the table in front of the chairs.

Carlotta perched on the edge of her desk. "I suppose I can say without violating confidentiality, Lieutenant, that the firm is, indeed, a party to these proceedings. I am prepared to cooperate whenever possible in bringing to justice the individual who so brutally ended the life of Ninon Bilyeu. She was a saint like these parts have never before known."

Not expecting a frank and favorable prelude to their discussion, he was left a little off-kilter, having planned a line of inquiry geared to wheedle as much out of her as he could vis-à-vis Ninon Bilyeu's will or any other facts she might have at her disposal. "Ms. Humphrey, that is most, uh, most reassuring." He sat back in his chair. "I mean, uh, knowing that you and I have the same goal— to discover and bring to justice, as you said, Sister Clare's assailant."

"You must understand our firm has represented the Bilyeu family for many years. Anything short of our most enthusiastic participation in this endeavor would be indefensible."

She must have really meant it, he concluded, though she'd rattled it off as if she were speaking into an audio voice recorder. "Ms. Humphrey," he said, then paused. Given the informality of her pose, he expected to hear *call me Carlotta*, which he did not. "I am just, uh, so—"

"Now, don't tell me you anticipated resistance on our part."

Our? He inferred *the royal we*. According to his

source on all things Humphrey, after Ellis died, Carlotta had managed the law firm single-handedly. He cleared his throat. "No, I wasn't sure *what* your position might be, given attorney-client privilege. It can be a hindrance, well, in some cases I've handled, it's been a hindrance."

She reached for a crystal decanter on the far corner of the desk and poured herself a whiskey. Pointing a rock glass in his direction, she offered to pour him one, too.

"I'm on duty, ma'am, so I will have to decline, but thank you all the same. Maybe another time."

She moved to the chair across from his and unzipped her boots. "You don't mind, do you? They aren't broken in quite yet, and I cannot have them on my feet another second."

"Of course."

She raised her left leg in his direction. "Could you help me out here?"

Seeing no other way, he obliged, tugging at the left boot, then the right.

She thanked him and pushed the boots under her chair. "Now, then, please tell me how I can help."

"The most urgent matter, as I see it, is to attempt to establish a motive for the murder. In my experience, knowledge of the victim's resources is helpful, and in this case, the obvious course of action would be, uh, to take a look at the will."

Slipping on a pair of cat-eye readers, she picked up the document to which he'd referred and, scanning page by page, came to the relevant paragraph. "It's a rather simple document. As a consecrated virgin of the Order of the Poor Clares, Ninon Bilyeu, known as Sister Clare, had little of value, I'm guessing, other than her ancestral home, of course, Larkspur Plantation."

"Yes," he said, "that's what I anticipated."

She turned the page. "It wouldn't be in violation of the heirs' trust, whom I intend to contact right away, if I were to tell you that she has bequeathed her property to her closest relatives, Mr. A. B. Bilyeu of New Orleans, Louisiana, Mr. Cecil DeGroat of Memphis, Tennessee, and Ms. Emma Jackson, née DeGroat, of Savannah, Georgia."

He retrieved a pad and pencil from his lapel pocket and jotted down the names. "And perhaps you can tell me, if you know, what the value of the property might be."

"When last assessed, the worth was some four million dollars, but a new assessment will be required for tax purposes. The deceased specified as well that the buildings on the property go to Blanchard College." She glanced up. "With the condition, it says here, that they be restored and established as a museum."

"I see."

"Additionally, she stipulates that the remaining heirlooms—and she mentions here two dueling pistols and a jewel-encrusted dagger—are to go to St. Mary of the Angels, either to be kept as part of their treasure or put up for sale." Her brown eyes, lined by long, dark lashes, narrowed.

With her mention of the jewel-encrusted dagger, Carlotta had dealt him a royal flush. He put on his best poker face, intent on revealing nothing. "You wouldn't happen to know the exact *whereabouts* of the heirlooms, would you, Ms. Humphrey?"

She flipped from one page to the next. "Well, it doesn't say here, so I would assume that Ninon had them in her possession. She didn't have a bank vault, to my knowledge."

"They must be at the hermitage, then."

"Or the church." She sipped her drink. "According to the most recent assessment, provided by Abboud Antiques in June, 2000, these items are quite valuable." Her eyebrows lifted. "Yes, *quite* valuable."

"Might I ask *how* valuable?" He sat with his pencil poised to write.

"Close to two million dollars." She raised her eyes.

"Uh-*huh*." He jotted down the figure. "Is it, uh, not unusual, extraordinary, actually, for such valuable items to be kept in an unknown location?"

"Unwise, yes, but extraordinary?" Her lips curved cynically. "You'd be surprised." She reordered the pages and dropped the document on top of the stack of folders. "That's it. The house, the buildings, and some pricey heirlooms." She reached for her whiskey again.

"I don't suppose you would know, uh, if Sister Clare was ever involved in any kind of conflict."

"Conflict?" She swirled her drink as she thought.

"With her family, for example, and I guess I'd have to add the church."

She frowned and shook her head. "Not as far as I know, but for family history, you'd best get in touch with A. B. Bilyeu or his sister's children, Cecil and Emma. The Hembree and New Orleans branches of the family have been in fairly close touch since Mr. Jake's time. When Mr. Jake's son Arnold—Ninon's father—died, his cousin Emile saw to the property for some years. He was the first of the New Orleans Bilyeus to take an interest in Larkspur, well, since around the time of the Civil War."

"So the original owner was from New Orleans?"

"That's right," she nodded. "Daddy filled me in on

the salient details. Hershel Bilyeu and his wife Fernanda de Lobos arrived in Hembree about the time of the war, purchased land, built the old house—"

"The one in ruins?"

"Yes. The other buildings were constructed not too long after the main house. The old overseer's house later became the main house, and there's the shotgun cottages where a good number of sharecroppers lived."

"Hmm." He sat forward, tapping his pad against the table. "I'm wondering, Ms. Humphrey, if you are aware of any animosities, any that could have a bearing on the case."

"Certainly nothing recent. Mr. Arnold died a good thirty years ago, and by then, Ninon had already entered a convent."

"A crime of this nature, in which the victim—an eremitic nun, no less—is brutally stabbed…"

She shook her head. "Why would anyone—?"

"My point, precisely," he said. "Either she knew something the perpetrator didn't want revealed, or—"

"—somebody wanted to get ahold of her property."

"I can think of no other motive. Can you?"

She poured herself half a shot and sat gazing at the Bilyeu records, bulging with yellowed pages.

He waited for the Bilyeu sphinx (he liked to think of her that way) to proffer some astounding revelation. He tapped with his pad again. She said nothing. If she knew something that might be relevant to the crime, what would it take to tease it out of her? If not her client's murder, *por dios, ¿qué?*

He put his writing instrument back in his pocket and stood. "I don't want to keep you any longer. You've been most helpful."

"Of course, Lieutenant. I hope I—the will, that is—has shed some light on this situation."

"It's a piece of the puzzle, and I appreciate your willingness to share the information."

She tucked the document inside the top folder and stood. "All right, then. Let me show you out."

"One more favor?" He stepped back, allowing her to pass. "If Dot could provide me with the heirs' contact information, that would be helpful."

"Of course. I'll see she does, first thing tomorrow morning."

He followed her through the door. At the stairwell, she stopped and offered him her hand, which he shook and smiled back warmly. In this game of clues, she'd dealt him an important card, though she didn't seem to know it. "Mr. So-and-So did it at the hermitage with the victim's own jewel-encrusted dagger," he mumbled to himself, as he took by two the long flight of stairs that led to the Square.

Chapter Fourteen

Thursday, September 24, early morning
Hembree Police Station

Olivera got to the station early and headed straight
to his cubicle. He turned his desk calendar to the next
page and, tilting back, crossed his arms over his chest.
He was making progress with the first case, but now he
had a second. But a second what—murder investigation?
Skeletal remains insinuated foul play, yes, but he
couldn't say he had another murder on his hands, not for
sure. He'd have to wait for the coroner's report, which,
hopefully, would arrive by late afternoon.

His eyes shifted from the blank computer screen to
the bronze pyx. For a year he'd hardly noticed it—a mere
fixture on his desk, a souvenir of his final trip to the Santa
Clara mission. It wasn't just a whatnot, though—it had
its practicality. He muttered "practicality" and flipped
back the lid. Once it was practical, before he dumped the
contents into his top drawer. His lips twisted into a smirk.
His old super had slung that word in his face till it felt
like a slap. He was practical, *por dios*, but not to an
extreme. Wright's *hard, cold facts* held little appeal to
him, lacked texture—yes, that was the word. *Texture*. He
moved the pyx to the center of the desk. He fancied it
without pencils and markers. He picked it up and took a
closer look. The craftsman, in stippling the surface, had

illuminated *a particular element*. "Exactly, that's how it's done." Facts by themselves didn't give a distinctive structure to a crime. They had to be mottled, like objects on an engraver's plate, or interwoven, like fibers. As he saw it, the detective's job was to expose *the connections*, make sense of the relationships. He set the pyx down and, leaning back, raised his eyes toward the dingy ceiling, where a row of fluorescent lights flickered and buzzed. "Connections…"

He sat up straight and reached for the index card he'd propped against the pyx—his "map." He'd gathered some important information the afternoon before, at the overseer's house—the so-called summer house—and, later, at Carlotta Humphrey's office, but he hadn't added anything to the card. He'd hoped to arrive at a clearer notion of motive. Unfortunately, he had not. All he'd managed to establish was that Sister Clare's will was equitable. Equitable, yes. Her family, the church, the community at large… She'd spread her assets among the three of them, without slighting anyone. As far as he could see, none of the heirs had anything to beef about, but then again… He paused, tapping the card against the desk. *Greed was a powerful motivator.* He couldn't forget that. Hmm. Maybe the Bilyeus had expected to get it all. He also had to consider DeGroat's visit to the hermitage. He'd seen his cousin on the day she was killed. That he knew. But why? What was the reason for his going there? He picked up a pen and made a note: "Speak to DeGroat ASAP." Had he wanted to talk to Sister Clare about her will? Pressure her into changing it so as to exclude the church and the college, leave it all to the family? He somehow doubted that DeGroat would have killed for the heirlooms and a couple of run-down buildings. Not that killing her would have made any difference. Wouldn't have accomplished a thing. But who, then, would've had an axe to grind if not the family? He scratched his head.

He pulled out his handkerchief and buffed the pyx till it glistened. Then, he got up and approached the window at the back of his cubicle. A dumpster and a gravel parking lot—that was all he could see. It reminded him of that other dumpster in that last miserable case. Two bodies in a dumpster, a stone's throw from the Santa Clara mission. Galloway, a priest—ha! Sorry excuse for a man of the cloth. And if a priest could do *that*...well. But Galloway hadn't killed for money. His motive was different. He'd done it to shut the women up. His eyes focused away from the dumpster and toward the horizon, blue and cloudless, then drifted back to the dumpster. Could Sister Clare have known something? Something incriminating? About a family member, or Moody, or Mannix? Whom else might she have known something about? The Fergusons?

Repelled by the view, he moved away from the window, retreated to his chair. His map lay in front of him on the desk. He picked up a pen, ready to sketch— but what? As far as things physical were concerned, foremost in his mind was the dagger. McGinnis had theorized that a jewel-encrusted dagger—what a thought!—had made the wound in the victim's abdomen. Now, according to the will, she herself was likely in possession of such a weapon. He shook his head. It was all quite farfetched. But there it was, a bejeweled dagger as the murder weapon, and it was up to him to track it down. If the perp hadn't carried it off—illogical as that seemed—it ought to be on the grounds. A possibility, not a strong one, but a possibility all the same. He certainly couldn't rule it out.

It wasn't inside the hermitage—that much he knew. He and Springer had searched the place thoroughly. But they hadn't adequately searched the grounds. They'd have to go back. He made another note, then reached for the stack of snapshots Springer had left on his desk. Shuffling through, he came to a picture of the garden. "Yes," he muttered, "not a bad place to hide something." Turning the pictures over as he went, he came to a shot of the evergreens at the entrance, then the sunflower patch close to the death scene. "A handy hiding place for the murder weapon," he said. "Or would it be?" Probably not. Too close to the body. He continued going through the pictures until he came to one of the garden. Not the well-kept plot he would have imagined, it looked a bit overgrown, with sprawling squash plants, yellowing leaves. Moody said he'd seen her digging in the garden that morning, which seemed a bit strange, now that he thought about it. Didn't seem like the season for digging. Harvesting, yes, but digging? He and Springer would have to go back over there, scour the entire area for any sign of the heirlooms. A smile rippled across his face. If Sister Clare was leaving the heirlooms to St. Mary's, what reason would she have to hide them? Why not put them in the church for safe keeping? And if the dagger was, in fact, in the church, then Moody would've had access to the weapon. He'd have to question him again— yes, indeed—and right away. "No," he said, changing his mind, he wanted to talk first to Nadia Abboud, who'd seen the dagger and likely knew all about it, including where it was kept. He'd speak to her, then Moody. Moody...he didn't trust the man—why he wasn't sure.

He scrolled through his phone contacts and, coming to Nadia's number, tapped "call." "Ms. Abboud?"

"Yes, this is she."

"Lieutenant Olivera here. I wonder if I might drop by your shop this morning. I have a question or two concerning a case I'm working on, and it's come to my attention you provided an assessment, some time ago, I think it was, of certain items of interest."

"Items of interest?"

"Yes, but I'd prefer not to get into that just yet. Is now a good time?"

"Well, I'm pretty busy here, but I guess I could take a break."

"Then, you're available?"

"I suppose so."

"I'll be right over."

He picked up his hat and briefcase and, on his way out, stopped at the reception desk. "Ms. Hill."

"Yes, Lieutenant?" She put down the morning paper and looked up.

"I guess Springer hasn't made it in yet."

"Not yet."

"When he gets here, tell him I've gone to Abboud Antiques and that I need him to organize another search of the hermitage. I'll text him the details. Tell him to take Reagan along. I'll meet them there directly."

He went on foot to the antique shop, only a short block from the station and, finding the "closed" sign in place, rang the bell. Ms. Abboud answered promptly and invited him in—more cordially than she had done at their last encounter, when he'd come to collect items she'd purchased at the Hansbrough estate sale.

She laid her box opener on the counter and shoved a

carton with her foot. "Careful, Lieutenant, there're boxes everywhere. All this arrived in the morning's post. I'm so busy these days I can hardly stay on top of things."

"A busy time for the antiques business?"

"Everything in Hembree bustles this time of year, when people have got money in their pockets. Is this your first fall here?"

"No, as a matter of fact, it isn't. I arrived here in August a year ago. Seems longer."

"Well, I'm sure it does, but when you're settled in, make friends..." With the back of her hand, she brushed her long, dark hair away from her face, then waved him toward a pair of leopard parson's chairs. "Have a seat, won't you?"

After thanking her for seeing him on short notice, he explained the reason for his visit. "I've learned recently that Abboud Antiques assessed the value of certain items mentioned in Ninon Bilyeu's will."

"It's a possibility. We've done business with the Bilyeus off and on." She picked up a lavender porcelain teacup and sipped. "Can I offer you a cup of tea?"

He turned down her offer and continued. "You may recall, then, a pair of dueling pistols and a jewel-encrusted dagger."

"Must have been some time ago, but I can check the records. What exactly was it you wanted to know?"

He paused to consider how much he was prepared to reveal. "If you had, uh, a photograph or, if not, a detailed description would be helpful."

She opened the top drawer of a cabinet and thumbed through till she came to the Bilyeu file. "I imagine we'll find what you're looking for here." She pulled out a stack of photographs and shuffled through them. "Here we go,

Lieutenant." She set some black-and-white snapshots on the table between the chairs.

"Yes, this is exactly what I need, and, if you have no objection, I'd like to make copies."

"Not a problem, as long as you return them."

"Springer can drop them off, say, tomorrow?"

"Take more time if you need it—a week, say?"

He twisted the photographs of the dagger and pistols around for a better look, then picked up the assessment. "Could you tell me a bit about the history of these items? You must have researched them."

"Not I. Ninon's father requested the assessment, and my father took care of it. These items were passed down from the first Bilyeu settlers, Hershel Bilyeu and his wife Fernanda de Lobos."

"You're familiar with the family history, I see."

"Yes, of course." She took a seat in the vacant chair. "I didn't do the research, but my father went on and on. The Bilyeus are among our best clients. Not so much now, but in my father's time. He and Arnold were of the same generation. His great-grandparents arrived around the time of the Civil War and eventually established Larkspur Plantation. Europeans, they were; he, French, she, Spanish. But they came here from New Orleans. Arnold, Ninon's father, was the son of Jake, who was Hershel and Fernanda's only grandchild. When Jake died, Arnold inherited the estate. He must have passed the heirlooms on to Ninon."

"The value of these items is rather surprising to me." He glanced at the photographs on the table between them. "Perhaps you can explain?"

"I wouldn't be surprised if they're worth as much as the land."

111

"Not quite that much, but, yes, as you must know, two million or so."

She picked up the paperwork and turned to the notes clipped to the assessment. "These are not ordinary heirlooms. I can promise you that. They're seventeenth-century and at one time belonged to a Spanish monarch." She pointed to a name. "Carlos II, the last of the Spanish Hapsburgs."

He nodded. "Impressive, so, how did the Bilyeus come to have them in their possession, if you know?"

"Fernanda de Lobos," she said, then paused, her eyes flicking to the wall at the right of the counter. "We used to have her portrait over there." She pointed to an arrangement of blue porcelain plates hung above a marble-topped credenza. "She was a descendent of the Count of Lobos, who received his title from Carlos II. When the king bestowed the honor, he made the count a gift of the pistols and dagger, which accounts primarily for their value. But regardless of provenance, the dagger would be quite a treasure because of the bejeweled handle."

"May I see that again?"

She handed him the assessment, and he looked again at the description of the gemstones. "Color, limpidity, iridescence, and chatoyance..." He put the sheets on the table. "Your father is an expert, no?"

"Yes, not all antique dealers are, but gemstones are a specialty of his—and portraits."

"So, I suppose these aren't chips." He glanced back at the picture.

She laughed. "No, they're all faceted gems."

He slipped the photographs and paperwork into his briefcase, then said, "Would you happen to know where the heirlooms are kept?"

"I don't really know, but I suppose Arnold either kept them in a safe at the house or a bank box. While my father had them, he would've kept them in the safe, for sure. I have no idea where they are now."

"I wonder, Ms. Abboud, if it's generally known, uh, if people know these valuable items are *here*—in Hembree, I mean."

"As my father told it, his client didn't want anyone to know about them. I was only there at the house once, and that was after Arnold passed away. There were no heirlooms on display, at least not in the public rooms."

He glanced at the spot where the matriarch's portrait had hung. "You say you used to have a portrait of Fernanda de Lobos. Where is it now?"

"My father was quite fond of it, as was I. The painting was beautiful, rather unusual. He acquired it at the estate sale. Most of the items he bought went quickly, but he over-priced a few, hoping to keep them around for a while. Years later, someone came in looking for items from the estate. He bought the portrait and whatever else was left."

"Would you have a record of the sale?"

"When my father was working, he was a meticulous record keeper. I'm sure he kept records of all his sales. But that was some years ago."

"The records would be here in the shop?"

"Possibly," she said. "The older sales records are kept in the back room. I could check but I would need a little time."

"I would appreciate it very much if you could, uh, make that a priority?" He zipped his briefcase and leaned forward.

She gave him a searching look. "If you believe this could have a bearing on the case, of course, I'll do what I can."

He stood and placed his card on the counter. "If you come up with anything relevant, please give me a call." As he reached the door, he put on his hat, but instead of leaving, he looked back. "Those vases were returned to you?"

"Vases? Oh, of course." She stood and pointed to a pair of porcelain objects. "And there they sit."

"Probably worth a month's pay." He smiled.

"Possibly. Original Havilands are expensive. Only a collector would pay the price."

"Well, I don't have any furniture to speak of, so I don't need any accessories." He smiled again. "Thanks for seeing me on short notice. I won't take up any more of your time." He realized as he turned to go that his respect for Ms. Abboud had grown. She didn't seem at all the woman who'd gotten into a row with Springer over a couple of sequestered vases. She was pleasant, knowledgeable.

"Hope I've been of help. By the way, Lieutenant," she leaned against the counter, "there *is*, uh, one thing that may or may not have anything to do with this."

"What's that?"

"Well, it seems one of the Lobos relatives may be in Hembree."

He stared, not sure what to make of her revelation. "In Hembree, you say?"

"Yes, here in Hembree."

"You've met him, spoken with him?"

"Only briefly, yesterday, at the Tavernette. Mosey introduced him."

He sighed. Mosey, of course, who else? "And how is he related to the Lobos family?"

"I have no idea. But I do know that one of his family members, long dead now, was here around the time of the Depression."

"Where might I find this individual, this—"

"Rafael de Lobos."

He walked back to the counter, put down his briefcase, and pulled out his tablet. "Rafael de Lobos." He jotted down the name.

"I'm not sure where he's staying, but I could find out."

"Yes, please do." He reached for the card he had set on the counter and, striking through the office number, wrote down the number of his cell phone. "As soon as you know anything, give me a call, would you? This is my cell. I have it with me at all times." He handed her the card and, tipping his hat, left the store.

Chapter Fifteen

Thursday, September 24, morning
Road to Conakry, AR

After residing in Hembree for more than a year,
Olivera was finally warming up to the topography of the
Arkansas Delta. Yet, when he got out on the open road,
as when he drove the two-lane blacktop from Hembree
to Conakry or Hembree to Mound City, he marveled at
the flatness of the landscape, the scarcity of trees, the
vast quantity of sunlight that blanched the foliage and
undergrowth to a silvery green. The impoverishment of
the small river towns with their dilapidated houses and
businesses bewildered him. He couldn't fathom how a
hole-in-the-wall like the Roadway Bait Shop or the
Jeremiah Java Café managed to hang on month after
month, year after year.

As he neared Conakry, the thin, towering steeple of
St. Patrick's Catholic Church came into view, then its red
brick walls, solid and plain, only breached by diminutive
windows. He pulled into the parking lot next to a black
sedan and called up the Vehicle History Report. "Very
good," he mumbled. "The monsignor is, indeed, in." All
he'd managed to inveigle from his secretary's ramblings
was that *the monsignor might be in.*

He entered the foyer through the vaulted door, the
most lavish feature of the exterior. Engulfed in darkness,

he advanced toward the faint light of the sanctuary where suspended globes cast their radiance on the pews below. Finding the church empty, he rounded the building and came to a door that led to a room behind the sanctuary. He knocked. A tall, redheaded man, lean and white-faced, peered out at him.

"Monsignor Mannix? Sorry to disturb you, but your secretary said you might be in this morning."

"Come in, come in. You're letting out the cool air."

He entered the monsignor's office, which was as gothic, if not as dark, as the church. The desk was small and plain, a wooden platform without side panels or drawers. It was easier to imagine a monk on the bench behind it copying a manuscript with a quill than a twenty-first-century priest tapping at a keyboard. He removed his hat and held out his credentials. "Lieutenant Olivera, Hembree Police Department."

Mannix took a perfunctory glance, then sat down on the bench. "What brings you to Conakry, Lieutenant?"

Olivera settled into the armchair near the door. "Well, sir," he began, "as you might imagine, we're investigating the murder of Ninon Bilyeu, known as Sister Clare."

"Of course, you *would* be investigating that. Terrible loss."

"Everyone I've spoken with seems to think so. No one can imagine why anyone would have wanted her dead. Seems incredible."

"Yes, it does to me, too." His eyes fell.

"I spoke to Father Moody...uh, you know Father Moody."

"Yes, indeed, I do."

"He was nearby, at St. Mary of the Angels Church,

when she was stabbed. He administered or at least attempted to administer last rights." He paused. "The coroner had to intervene. Preserve the crime scene as best she could."

"I understand. Father Moody called me. Very upset. A great loss for Melvin."

"I have spoken with him, and he said that he was not Sister Clare's confessor. He said you, Monsignor, are, or rather were her confessor. Is that correct?"

"Yes, I knew her for a good many years before she assumed her commitment as an eremitic nun. It seemed proper I should continue in that capacity."

"It's a good little ride from here to Hembree. If you wouldn't mind my asking, did you hear her confession on a regular basis?"

"Somewhat regular. I saw her every few weeks."

"At the hermitage?"

"No, the confessional whenever possible."

"Whenever possible?"

"When the church wasn't occupied. When it was, I spoke with her at the hermitage."

"Forgive this question, which may seem strange, but did she keep anything of value at the hermitage?"

"No, of course, not," he said in a somewhat derisive tone, then threw up his hands. "What possessions would a Poor Clare have?"

"Well, now that you've asked," Olivera said, calm and collected, "a dagger with a bejeweled handle worth a million dollars, more or less."

Mannix stared back stony-eyed. "Have you found something of that nature at the hermitage?"

"We have reason to suspect *something of that nature* was on the premises but seems to have gone missing."

"I know nothing about that."

"You are aware, Monsignor, that Sister Clare was stabbed. No doubt about it."

"That's what Melvin told me. But with a bejeweled dagger? He said nothing about that."

"He wouldn't have known, would he? Unless, of course— Well, never mind that." He cleared his throat. "I know the confessional is sacrosanct, but, given the circumstances, I wonder if Sister Clare might have said anything to you, uh, to suggest she was embroiled in a conflict, a difference of opinion that might have caused her to feel threatened?"

"To an outsider, she might have seemed isolated, vulnerable, but I assure you she was not." He punctuated his answer with a slight harrumph.

The priest's reaction prompted Olivera to remember the pyx and how the iconic Sister Clare had protected her convent with the consecrated host. "I think I know what you mean."

"Are you Catholic, Lieutenant?"

"I was raised Catholic."

"Then you know that those who serve the Lord are not fearful."

His tone was stern, maybe a little too stern. Was Mannix himself fearful? And if so, of what? He pulled his tablet and pencil from his lapel pocket and opened to a fresh page. "Let me return to something you said before, uh, that you've known Sister Clare for many years. I believe that's what you said, isn't it?"

"That's right. I met her at Perpetual Adoration. It's a convent north of here."

"She must have been very young."

"She was."

"And then both of you moved to the same area. Would you be able to say anything about her decision to leave the convent, seclude herself at the hermitage?"

He shifted on his bench. "I may have had something to do with that."

"How's that?"

"Well, I encouraged her to follow her inclinations, to live a deeply spiritual life, somewhat different from what is customary for nuns."

"Sister Clare was born in Hembree. Her family must have been glad for her return."

"Her family? I don't believe she had any family in Hembree. Her parents were dead, and she was an only child."

"So, her father had already died when she moved to the hermitage?"

"Yes."

"You wouldn't remember when that was exactly?"

"The mid-eighties, I believe."

"And did you leave your assignment before or after Sister Clare came to Hembree?"

"I'm not sure how any of this could relate to your investigation." Mannix shook his head with impatience. "Surely this murder has nothing to do with Sister Clare's religious life."

"When a person with minimal contacts, like Sister Clare, is murdered, it is difficult to know where to begin. There's no family to speak of. Distant cousins scattered about the region. Where do you suggest I look?"

"I'm afraid I can't help you." He threw up his hands again. "I'm as puzzled as you are."

Olivera took a card from his pocket and placed it on the desk. "If you should remember something that might help us, please call."

"I can't imagine what that would be, but, of course, if I should think of something."

"Thank you for your time."

Once out the door, Olivera glanced at his watch. He was meeting Springer and Reagan at the hermitage at two o'clock. He'd have to hurry. He took off, churning up enough gravel to bring the monsignor out of his office and into the parking lot. Olivera waved as he pulled away. But Mannix, ignoring his gesture, got into his car and pulled off in the opposite direction.

Chapter Sixteen

Thursday, September 24, early afternoon
Road from Conakry to Hembree

Olivera was halfway back to Hembree, past Gideon but not quite to Jenkins, when his phone rang. Frye, Frye, and Humphrey appeared on the screen. He tapped the "accept" button. "Ms. Humphrey, what can I do for you?"

"Hello, Lieutenant. I wanted to let you know that Ninon's relatives arrived last night. They're here to bury their cousin."

"You know where they're staying?"

"They're at the Tavernette."

"I'm not sure we're ready to release the body," he said.

"I spoke with Eads, and she says we need your signature, that's all."

"Let me speak to Dr. McGinnis first."

"Might that be today?"

"I'll do my best."

"By the way," she said, "I've looked at the Bilyeu records, and something doesn't seem quite right. Could you stop by the office late today or early tomorrow?"

"I'll make it a priority." He heaved a sigh.

"Text or call me when you get a minute, please, sir."

He clicked off and ran through his mental agenda.

Meet Springer and Reagan at the hermitage, interview Bilyeu and DeGroat, speak with McGinnis, and now, stop by the law firm.

He arrived at the hermitage and spotted Springer and Reagan at work in the deceased nun's garden. "Find anything?" he called.

Springer sank the tip of his shovel in the soil, then rested his elbow on the handle. "Yep—not sure exactly what."

Olivera made his way through sprawling vines and end-of-the-season cucumbers that lay withering in the midday heat.

"We've searched every inch, Chief, just like you said, and this is all we turned up." He took a handkerchief from his back pocket and wiped his face.

"Every inch," Reagan echoed.

Springer gestured toward a small trunk, then stepped back from the hole and leaned his shovel against the side of the cottage.

"Uh-*huh*." Olivera picked up the shovel and scraped the top. "I knew there'd be something here. A trunk, eh? Looks like a trunk. You haven't tried to lift the lid?"

"Nope," Reagan said. "Waitin' for you, Lieutenant."

"Well, I suppose we need to get it to the lab. Might as well pull it out of the ground."

Springer and Reagan loosened the soil around the trunk and, grabbing it by the handles, lifted it out of the hole.

"Hold on, Springer," Reagan said. "What's that?"

Olivera looked into the hole. "Not sure, but it looks to me like a metal box. You'll need to dig that out, too. Actually, you two take the trunk to the van while I see what we've got here." He broke up the earth around the object, then slipped on a pair of gloves and knelt next to the hole. He thumped the top with his forefinger. "Metal, for sure."

Springer approached. "What you got, Chief?"

"Looks like a cash box. Too bad it's locked. You didn't find any keys around here, did you?"

Springer shook his head. "We could check again in the hermitage."

"Good idea." Olivera got to his feet. "Reagan, come get this and put it in the van. Springer, you come with me."

Olivera pushed back the door to the hermitage. "You take the left side. I'll take the right." He pointed to the armoire in the back corner. "Might as well start with that."

Olivera approached the table. A table drawer, he thought, might be a likely place for a key. He pulled it out and turned it over. Papers, cards, and trinkets spilled out but no key. He examined the bed, a wooden frame with leather straps, but again, he found nothing. "Did you check the bookcase?"

"Not yet." Springer pulled a pair of black walking shoes from the armoire and shook them. "Nothing here, Chief."

"A devoted reader might hide a key in a book." Olivera pulled up a chair and lugged books off the bottom shelf, religious books mostly, except for a manual on gardening. The metal box was in the garden... so, she might have hidden the key in a book on gardening. Makes sense. He flipped the pages and out dropped a key. "Found it." He held it up for Springer to see, then fell silent. "You didn't see signs of digging anywhere else in the garden?"

"Didn't miss a row, Chief. The ground's hard as a rock, pure buckshot, but somebody'd been digging in the back corner."

"Take one last look, will you?"

Springer walked back to the garden, while Olivera headed to the van, where Reagan stood guard over the day's findings.

"Okay, Reagan, we're through here. When Springer finishes, you and he get these items into evidence. See if this key doesn't fit the cash box. I'm in a bit of a rush— got to get over to the Tavernette. I'll see you back at the station."

Chapter Seventeen

Thursday, September 24, Happy Hour
The Tavernette

Olivera entered the Tavernette through the bar and tipped his hat to the hostess, who, as always, was zipped tightly into a black sheath, her frosted curls swept up into an unkempt knot. Lured by a rhinestone brooch, his eyes fell involuntarily on her décolletage. He cleared his throat, then glanced away and back before addressing the establishment's *grande dame*. "Ms. Tisdale, you've got a couple of guests here, A. B. Bilyeu and Cecil DeGroat. Would you mind giving them a call?"

"I'd be glad to, Lieutenant." She nodded and smiled.

Happy hour had begun, and the bar was buzzing. Taking the only vacant stool at the bar, he called to the waitress, "Ruby, could you bring me a club soda, please, ma'am?"

"Right away, Lieutenant. Can I get you something to nibble on—chips and salsa, chicken wings, fried mozzarella?"

"No, ma'am, just a club soda."

He flicked away the previous customer's crumbs and placed his map, i. e., index card, on the counter. He'd already sketched in Sister Clare's garden, not as it was now but as Springer's snapshot pictured it. Short his markers, he'd have to imagine the pile of dirt in the back corner and the trunk and cash box next to the hole. Anxious to see the contents of the containers, he planned to head to the station after speaking with the deceased's cousins. On second thought, maybe he'd stop by Frye, Frye, and Humphrey, then head to the station. He was just as anxious to find out *qué diablos* Carlotta meant by *something of interest*. Perhaps she'd come across the name of the victim or the perp. He felt sure the Larkspur records contained one or the other if not both.

"Lieutenant, can I start you a tab?"

He looked up, picking up his card. "What was that?"

"A tab. Shall I start you a tab?"

"No, ma'am, I'm good."

After wiping the counter, she set a glass of ice in front of him and snapped open a club soda.

He tossed a few crumpled dollar bills on the bar, then picked up his drink. He took a sip and stared out the window at the brick sidewalk that ran in front of the Tavernette and around the square. Catty-cornered from the pub stood Frye, Frye, and Humphrey. With crape myrtles blocking his view, he could see only part of the building. Around the corner on Lexington was Nadia Abboud's shop. Had she been able to find the name of the man who purchased the Fernanda de Lobos portrait? She'd be closing soon, maybe meeting her sidekick Mosey, uh-huh. He chuckled. His *allies*. He'd hardly heard a peep out of Mosey since the investigation began, but she was there all right, probably hatching a plot with Nadia, Saffron, or Carlotta—or all three.

Allies and suspects. He sipped his soda. Moody and Mannix. Hmm. Suspects or allies? Neither of them had taken Sister Clare's death exceptionally hard. But who had, come to think of it, if not Frank Sr.? He'd found the body, known her the longest—since she was a kid. But Mannix, her confessor, her long-time mentor, wouldn't he be upset, angry? Ally or suspect? And now he was about to add two more names to his list. A. B. Bilyeu and Cecil DeGroat. They were Ninon's distant cousins—but what else? Allies or suspects?

"Lieutenant Olivera?"

He put down his glass and looked at the man who'd spoken his name. He was tall, slim, dressed in a double-breasted suit—a Fendi or, if not, a good knock off. His hair was straight and dark, pulled back in a ponytail. "Mr. DeGroat?"

"Yes, and this is my uncle, Antoine Bilyeu." He stepped aside to reveal an older, plumper version of himself.

"Shall we move to a quieter spot?" the older man said.

"Yes, let's go to the dining room." Olivera pointed the way. "Would you care for something to drink?"

"Care for anything, Uncle Antoine?"

"I could drink a Bloody Mary, I expect."

"Two Bloody Marys." Olivera laid a bill on the counter before following his *persons of interest* to the corner near the front window.

"This spot good, Lieutenant?"

He nodded, and DeGroat pulled out chairs for the three of them. "Appreciate your agreeing to meet. I know you're here to make your cousin's funeral arrangements. My condolences to you both."

"Thank you, Lieutenant. I can't begin to express my shock," DeGroat said, taking a seat. "I was with her just days ago at the hermitage. I couldn't have imagined—"

"Sudden and horrific," Bilyeu said, eyes downcast.

He sat with some difficulty, then settled his spindly legs, one then the other, under the table.

"Did you know Sister Clare well?" Olivera glanced at Bilyeu, then DeGroat. "It's my understanding, having spoken with Ms. Humphrey, that the Hembree Bilyeus have been in touch with the Louisiana Bilyeus only in the last few years. Is that correct?"

"Well, yes and no," Bilyeu said. "The two sides of the family went their separate ways for a time. That part's true. But after Arnold, Ninon's father, passed, Emile, my older brother, took charge of the farm."

"So you knew Ninon well?"

"No, not well. Ninon left home early, entered a convent near Memphis—or was it Helena? Not sure about that. Somewhere north of here."

"The truth of the matter," DeGroat said, "is we were in touch but not close. Ninon was my fourth cousin. I'd never met her, sad to say, until this week."

"I see."

Bilyeu sat forward. "There was the land to consider, Lieutenant, *the land*, Hershel's estate." His voice, at full volume, resounded in the empty room. "Hershel Bilyeu. Surely you've heard speak of him...the first successful planter around here. Turned a swamp into a gold mine."

"Would you say, then, that your interest was primarily of a business nature?"

Bilyeu stiffened.

"We wouldn't have put it that way," DeGroat said, "but if you insist, yes, I would say that our interest is primarily in preserving the estate."

"Would you mind describing for me the purpose of your recent visit?"

"Not at all. I came here, on the family's behalf, to

ask Ninon if Uncle Antoine and I might take up where Uncle Emile left off. Cultivate the land, restore the buildings. She'd taken a vow of poverty. Wouldn't profit from the venture. But her order might have appreciated an annual contribution." He crossed his legs, drawing Olivera's attention to a pair of sleek, black Poitiers.

"Did she accept your proposition?"

"Yes, she did. You see, all this would've happened anyway, and Ninon was glad to see it happen *now* rather than later, after she was gone."

"Gone?" Olivera's eyes narrowed.

"Yes, that's what she said, *after she was gone.* The land would come to us, eventually, but she wanted to see Larkspur functioning again. She said she'd have to amend her will, since she'd left the buildings to Blanchard College."

"But, according to the document I've seen, the buildings *will* go to the college."

"Obviously," Bilyeu intruded, gray eyes glistening, "she didn't get a chance to change the will. That same day she was *murdered.*" He flopped one plump, manicured hand over the other.

Olivera flinched and cleared his throat. "Let's go back, uh, to that day, if you don't mind."

Ruby arrived with the Bloody Marys, which she set before Bilyeu and DeGroat. "Can I get you anything else, gentlemen?"

"You might bring me another one of these." Olivera set his empty glass on her tray and, smiling, waiting for her to depart. As soon as she had, he turned to DeGroat. "The day of the murder, if you could fill me in."

"It was all pretty cut and dry. I flew in around noon, rented a car, and drove out to the hermitage."

"Your cousin was expecting you?"

"Of course, I let her know I was coming."

"And you spoke to her at the hermitage?"

"That's right."

"And she was in agreement with your proposal concerning Larkspur."

"Yes, as I said before."

"And she said it would require a change in her will."

"Yes."

Olivera sat thinking, then said to DeGroat, "Were you concerned there might be opposition?"

"Not at all. If the college was aware of her bequest—and I'm not sure they were—I doubt they would have opposed a change. They wouldn't have had grounds."

"She mention any other aspect of the will besides the part about the land and the buildings?"

"If you're referring to the heirlooms, no, she did not." DeGroat stirred his drink with a celery stalk and took a sip. "But now that we've *seen* the will..."

"It seems," Olivera said, "Ninon was in possession of two dueling pistols and a bejeweled dagger, which Abboud Antiques assessed as worth in the neighborhood of two million dollars."

"We had no knowledge of that part of the will, Lieutenant, I can assure you."

Olivera's eyes moved from nephew to uncle to nephew. "Since Ninon had no opportunity to amend her will, those items will go to St. Mary of the Angels."

DeGroat nodded.

"They must have belonged to the Bilyeu family at one time," Olivera conjectured.

"Maybe they did belong to the Bilyeu family," the older gentleman said with conviction, "but not the New

Orleans Bilyeus, who are French Bourbon, *not* Spanish Hapsburg."

Olivera blinked. "Yes, I'm aware of the distinction." He stretched back, then continued. "The dagger and pistols were gifts to the first Conde de Lobos from the last Spanish Hapsburg king, Carlos II—or so I'm told." He took a sip of his drink. "Then *how*—?"

"Old rumors," Bilyeu interrupted, "*very* old rumors that have nothing to do with the subject at hand, seem to imply that Hershel's wife, who undeniably was a Lobos, might have *taken possession* of certain heirlooms before she and Hershel left New Orleans." He lifted his glass again and, before drinking, added, "That's all."

Olivera reached in his pocket for his tablet and turned to the notes he'd taken earlier that day. "George Abboud, who assessed the heirlooms at Arnold Bilyeu's request, kept Fernanda de Lobos's portrait at his antique shop for a good while, till it was purchased, according to his daughter Nadia, by an individual who came to the store hoping to find items left from the estate sale."

To Olivera's remark, nephew and uncle returned indifferent stares.

"These items," Olivera said, "pistols and a dagger that belonged to the Lobos family originally, at some point became part of the Hembree Bilyeu estate."

"I'm not sure what *other* conclusion one might draw." Drinking to the bottom of his glass, Bilyeu waved to a passing waitress. "Miss—"

DeGroat ordered another round for his uncle and himself and then turned to Olivera. "Neither of us has any objection to the stipulations of the current will. The important thing is we can now get the farm up and running again. We did, indeed, have plans for the buildings, and, of course, we will approach the college about a possible compromise. As for the heirlooms, if Ninon wanted them to go to St. Mary's, that was her prerogative."

Olivera sat listening to DeGroat and, when he'd finished, tapped gently on the rough surface of the table. "No objection, no objection at all?"

"We certainly have no objection."

"Someone *must* have objected." Olivera drummed the table with his fingertips. "And *who*, gentlemen, is what I need to know."

"Who *would* object?" Bilyeu retorted.

"Yes, exactly." Olivera looked at one, then the other.

"The college or the church, I suppose," DeGroat said. "But I'm not convinced—"

"Of course," Olivera cut in, "if the perpetrator's motive was greed…"

"What else?" Bilyeu said, with a waggle of his head. Having figured it out to his own satisfaction, apparently, he seemed annoyed at Olivera's speculations.

"Oh," Olivera said with a smile, "even when wealth *appears* to eclipse other motives, I always consider the possibility—"

"But, in this case, Lieutenant, what other motive could there be?" Bilyeu said.

Olivera opened his palms outward in a smooth gesture. "*Dozens* of motives, backed up by *mounds* of statistics. Hatred, jealousy, revenge, personal vendetta. I could go on and on."

The beads of sweat that had formed on the older man's forehead trickled down the sides of his face.

Ruby arrived with fresh Bloody Marys and a small

bowl of pretzels.

Olivera held the bowl toward Bilyeu and DeGroat before taking one himself. "I'm going to let you men drink your cocktails in peace. But before I go, I have a couple of quick questions for *you*, Mr. DeGroat. What time was it when you left the hermitage?"

"Two or two-thirty, maybe. Not any later."

"So between two and sixish?"

"I drove to Larkspur, strolled around the property, took some pictures of the buildings. Then I left for the airport, turned in the rental car, grabbed a sandwich at the snack bar, and waited for clearance."

"You didn't speak to anyone, see anyone?"

"Other than airport personnel, no, not that I recall."

"And as you left the hermitage, you didn't see anyone, meet anyone along the road?"

"Well, I wasn't really paying attention. I suppose I might have driven past a car or two, and, of course, farm vehicles."

"In case you think of anything." Olivera passed DeGroat his card. He stood and shook hands. "If you'd drop by the police station soon as possible, Mr. DeGroat, my sergeant will take your prints."

As Olivera left, more Tavernette *aficionados* pushed in, seemingly eager to get to their first alcoholic beverage of the day. He felt the same compulsion, but before he could settle down with a drink, he needed to see Carlotta, stop by the station, and, if time permitted, the morgue.

He crossed the square from corner to corner and, opening the street door to the law firm, came face to face with Ms. Humphrey.

"Lieutenant Olivera."

"Sorry I wasn't able to make it here sooner. *Very* full

day."

"I imagine so."

"But if you have a minute…"

"Certainly," she said. "Would you want to have a drink at the Tavernette? I'm headed in that direction."

"No, ma'am, sorry. I've just come from there, and I'm in a hurry to get back to the station."

"Well, what I called about wasn't all that important. It's just that when I was rummaging through the files, I came across the wills of several of Ninon's ancestors. All of them mentioned the land and the buildings, but not a one said a word about the heirlooms."

"Well, now, that *is* odd." He removed his hat and fanned his face.

"Yes, I thought so."

He stepped into the shade of the building. "Why, I wonder."

"That, Lieutenant, I couldn't tell you for sure, but my guess is they didn't want anyone to know. Seems obvious, don't you think?"

"And, of course, they *wouldn't* want anyone to know."

Her forehead wrinkled. "Why is that?"

"Well, according to rumor, mind you, they were stolen."

"Stolen?" Her brow lifted.

"Yes, I've been speaking with Mr. Bilyeu and Mr. DeGroat, and according to Mr. Bilyeu, Hershel's wife Fernanda took possession of those particular heirlooms before she and her husband left New Orleans."

"Well, that would explain—"

"Indeed, it would."

"Stolen heirlooms, kept hidden but passed down."

"Of course," he added, "we can't be *sure* they were stolen, can we? But it would be worth looking into." He was in no hurry to bring up the subject of Rafael de Lobos, so, for the moment, he kept that revelation to himself.

"Not that I would try to insinuate myself into your investigation, Lieutenant—"

Huh! Of course, she wouldn't, was his silent dig, accompanied by an imaginary eyeroll.

"—but if you run across anything of significance, related to the heirlooms, please let me know."

"Certainly," he said, then checked his watch again. "I'm sorry to have kept you standing here on the street. I need to get to the station. My staff will want to leave. But thank you for sharing that information, and if you should come across anything else—"

"I'll call."

He put on his hat, smiled at Ms. Humphrey, and hurried along Lexington toward the station.

Chapter Eighteen

Thursday, September 24, 6:00 p.m.
Hembree Police Station

By the time Olivera reached the station, it was close to six o'clock. Loud talk came from the right back corner of the building. Springer and Reagan were still there.

He pushed open the door to the evidence room and strode in. "Uh-huh, gentlemen. What have we here?"

Springer moved aside, allowing him full view of the contents of the trunk and cash box.

"Nicely arranged, Springer." He approached the dagger first. "My, my, the murder weapon itself." He thumped on the table beside the remarkable piece, in need of a good cleaning but impressive all the same. "But, of course, we'll need Dr. McGinnis to confirm." He slipped on a pair of latex gloves, then pulled out his recorder. "Uh-huh," he said, as he clicked it on, "one jewel missing and an oval-shaped aperture close in size to the opal Dr. McGinnis discovered near the wound. The blade's been wiped clean, looks like. However, on closer inspection," he said, then paused to pick up a magnifying glass, "small amounts of what appears to be blood remain on the handle and along the blade." He turned off the recorder and looked at Springer. "The dagger was in the trunk, I'm assuming."

"Right. The dagger on top, the pistols, underneath."

"Have the pistols been fired? You test for residue?"

Springer answered with a nod, and Reagan, standing sentry-like at the end of the table, added, "We sure did, Lieutenant, but there wasn't a trace of powder on either of 'em."

He turned to Springer again. "Anything else in the trunk?"

"Nothing but the cloth the dagger was wrapped in."

"And the cash box?"

"You won't believe this." Reagan eagerly called his attention to a leather-bound volume. It wasn't lying on the table but standing upright beside the box. It was open, and on the inside cover, there was a drawing of a skeleton. It wasn't exactly a book, since it didn't have any pages, only the drawing and, across from it, two vertical rows of drawers labeled with Latin inscriptions. Suspended between the rows of drawers was a small green bottle, held in place by a clamp.

"You ever seen one of these?" Reagan said.

"I have, actually, but certainly not in an evidence room."

"Mind telling us what it is?" Springer said.

"It's what was called an apothecary. A collection of herbs, chemicals, that sort of thing. Very old, centuries old, if I had to guess."

"What do you make of it, Lieutenant?" Reagan said.

"Well, I'm not sure what to make of it. I guess we can assume that it belonged to Sister Clare since it was buried together with these other items. Maybe another heirloom? A dandy piece of evidence, for sure, but I can't imagine how it figures in the case." He shrugged and closed the apothecary, then took a look at the exterior, hoping to find an engraving that would identify the owner. "No name, no initials." He took off his gloves. "Good job, men, and I need you to do one more thing for me before you go. Pack the items individually, out of their containers—but take the containers, too—label them all, and get them over to the morgue. I want Dr. McGinnis to see all this as soon as possible."

"Certainly, Chief," Springer said.

"We've got another suspect coming in for prints, Cecil DeGroat, who, turns out, is Sister Clare's fourth cousin. He was at the crime scene sometime before the murder occurred—or so he claims. Get finger and shoe prints and a swipe. His phone number is on file."

"The guy in the prop plane?" Springer said.

"The same."

Olivera left the evidence room and walked to his cubicle, cell phone in hand. He dropped down into his chair and called McGinnis.

"Lieutenant."

"Glad I caught you. We've uncovered some rather spectacular evidence at the crime scene. Springer and Reagan are packing it up now. If you can stick around for half an hour or so…?"

"No problem, I'll be here."

"Good. I'll get over there as soon as I can. And by the way, any progress on the remains from the cistern?"

"Not yet."

"Well, we can get to that later, but these recent findings—"

"Okay. I'll take a look soon as they get here."

When Olivera arrived at the morgue a while later, Springer and Reagan were briefing McGinnis.

"The ground was pure buckshot," Springer said, as he helped himself to a cup of coffee, "except for that one area. So, we dug it up, me and Reagan, and when the chief got there, we lifted out the trunk. Then we spotted the cash box."

"So, all of this was in the garden, buried?" She eyed the objects strewn across the counter.

"That's right." Springer dropped a sugar cube in his cup.

"Late in the day for coffee, isn't it Springer?" Olivera said, approaching the counter.

Springer sniffed and dropped in another.

"You guys can go now. I appreciate your staying late. You contacted Mr. DeGroat, I'm assuming?"

"I did," Springer said. "He'll be at the station first thing tomorrow morning."

"Good work, men. See you bright and early." He nodded to them both.

"Okay, Chief," Springer said as he backed away. "Bright and early." His expression fell. "Oh, and thanks for the coffee, Dr. McGinnis."

"Any time, Sergeant."

The door closed, and Olivera directed his attention first to the dagger and then McGinnis. "Certainly not what one expects to find."

"No, I have *never*—"

"Nor have I," he responded. "Does the dagger match up with the wound?"

"We'll know soon enough." She unzipped the body bag and held the plastic-wrapped dagger against the abdomen. "The bruising here and here is consistent with the size and shape of the handle. And the length of the blade matches the depth of the wound. So, yes, this *could* be it, but I'll need to take some measurements."

"The setting of the missing jewel looks about the

size and shape of the opal that was in the wound, wouldn't you say?" His eyes searched the counter for whatever she might have done with the opal.

"It's in here." She retrieved a bottle from the evidence box, extracted the opal with tweezers, and lowered it into the empty setting. "I'd say that's a perfect fit."

"At last, *something* fits," he said with a sigh.

"I'll need to match the blood stains to the victim's blood type—"

"—and look for DNA." He moved away from the counter and, passing the gurney, pulled a handkerchief from his back pocket and wiped his eyes.

"Formalin?" she said.

He nodded. "Can't seem to get used to it." He sat in the chair next to the desk. "The perpetrator himself or herself must have stabbed the victim, then put the dagger back in the trunk. Father Moody said he'd seen Sister Clare digging in her garden earlier in the day."

"So, we might assume she could have dug up the trunk." She closed the evidence box and, joining him, perched on the edge of her desk.

"Given what I've just learned from Cecil DeGroat, who saw her shortly before she was murdered, I can see why she might have done that. DeGroat and his uncle wanted to take over the farm, get it running again, and Ninon was pleased about that, even suggested she would need to change her will so as to leave the land *and* the buildings to them. She'd originally left the buildings to the college." He'd been staring ahead as he talked, but now he stopped and faced McGinnis directly. "Maybe, just maybe, she changed her mind about the heirlooms."

"Why would she do that?"

"Good question. Why would she?" He looked away.

"Who's going to inherit the heirlooms?"

"According to the current will, the church gets the dagger and pistols. But the apothecary isn't mentioned. Strange, since it must be worth a good bit." He frowned and rubbed his chin.

"Ten thousand, fifteen, maybe."

"Which doesn't hold a candle to the other items, but still…" He stood, slipping both hands into his pockets. "Dr. McGinnis, know what? We may have just stumbled onto a motive." His eyes shifted from the coroner to the corpse. "Let's say the killer finds out Ninon is planning to change her will—"

"—which would eliminate DeGroat as a suspect. He had everything to gain and nothing to lose."

"Yes, that's right. If she'd gotten the chance, she'd have left the buildings to her cousins and that would have meant a loss for the college but not a personal loss. Of course, we only have DeGroat's word on that, but it makes sense. The heirlooms, on the other hand, were never mentioned—or so he claims. In fact, he and Bilyeu didn't seem at all interested in the heirlooms."

She opened her mouth, as if to speak.

He held up a hand. "Hold on a second. What if Ninon told Father Moody she'd decided not to leave the heirlooms to the church? Maybe she had a change of heart, decided her family ought to have them."

"You aren't suggesting, Lieutenant, that Father Moody—"

"Well…if not Moody, perhaps the monsignor."

"I can't imagine either of them stabbing Sister Clare for a dagger and pair of pistols, regardless of their value." She stood and approached the gurney. "And same as with the buildings, it wouldn't have meant a *personal* loss. Religious take a vow of poverty, do they not?"

"Yes," he said, "I think they do. It *is* hard to imagine, I grant you that."

"Not only that," she said, "if Father Moody wanted the heirlooms, why didn't he just *take* them when he had the chance?"

"You mean, supposing he got hold of the dagger?"

"Yes."

"Well, of course, because…because—"

"Maybe he heard something, took off—"

"Possibly," he said. "But if he was in that much of a hurry, how could he have cleaned the dagger, put it back in the trunk, and reburied it?"

"Excellent point."

He watched as she zipped the body bag and pushed the gurney into its niche. "Too bad corpses can't tell us everything we want to know."

"Oh, I don't know, Lieutenant." She closed the door to the mortuary cabinet. "They tell us a lot, considering they're dead. That one confirmed the weapon."

"But not the killer."

"So, we move on to the next piece of evidence."

"Where to start?" He stared down at the floor.

"The pistols?"

"We didn't find any residue on either one," he said.

"They were buried with the dagger, right?"

"Yes, the pistols and the dagger were buried inside the trunk, and I suppose that explains the inordinate amount of—what was it?"

"*Clostridium tetani*?"

"Yes."

"There doesn't appear to be any soil *inside* the

trunk," she said, "but if someone removed the dagger, then dropped it on the ground—"

"Yes, it could have happened that way." He paused, then sauntered back to the center of the room. "What about this? Ninon decides to bury the heirlooms, since there wasn't any safe place for them in the hermitage. The armoire didn't even have a lock."

"I suppose, but you have to wonder why objects of such value wouldn't have been kept in a safe or a bank vault."

"That would be the normal thing to do. Valuable things, irreplaceable things, are generally kept, as you say, in a safe or a bank vault. *But*...there is something that isn't normal here." As he spoke, his puzzlement was starting to clear. "We're certain the pistols and dagger are heirlooms. And yet the Bilyeus, with the exception of Ninon, didn't make mention of them in their wills."

"That *is* odd," she said.

"Yes and no. You see, the Bilyeus were *not* the rightful owners."

She frowned in obvious confusion.

"Fernanda de Lobos, Hershel Bilyeu's wife, brought them to Hembree clandestinely—get it? They ought to have stayed in New Orleans with the rightful heir to the Lobos title."

"Who was...?"

"The heir?" He shrugged. "Fernanda's father or grandfather...or brother, maybe, if she had a brother."

"So, the Bilyeus hid them, because they weren't legally theirs?"

"I'm assuming that, and Sister Clare, by naming them in her will, was the first Bilyeu ready to admit to their ownership."

"Admit, huh, but only after she was dead."

"Hmm." He paced again and vigorously rubbed his forehead. "She must have been of two minds."

She nodded, apparently following him now.

"She kept them buried and never alluded to their whereabouts in her will. And yet—"

"But Sister Clare," she interrupted, "wasn't much like her relatives, was she?"

"No, not at all. She reminds me, in fact, of another Sister Clare."

"What other Sister Clare?"

"The one Santa Clara, California was named for. Both nuns were from wealthy families, but, at an early age, renounced privilege to lead a life of poverty and seclusion."

"As a nun, her objectives would have been spiritual, not mundane. So, if she knew the heirlooms were stolen, she would have done what any good Catholic—"

"Any good Catholic—yes, of course. She would have wanted to make restitution."

"Exactly."

He took a seat on a metal stool and stretched his legs out in front of him. "What was her obligation, then? Could she have left them to St. Mary's or would she have been required to leave them to their rightful owner— whoever that might have been? I wonder how her spiritual mentor would have advised her on that?"

"Monsignor Mannix, you mean."

"I'll have to speak to the monsignor again, see if he can help sort this out. Though before when I talked to him, he claimed he knew nothing about any heirlooms."

She approached the book, which was lying in the spot where he'd left it. "This apothecary, I suppose it was an heirloom, too."

"It seems so, at least it was buried with the dagger and pistols, but in a separate case underneath the trunk." He slipped on gloves and removed the book from its plastic casing. "I've only seen one of these, and that was at the Apothecary Museum in New Orleans. We know a little about the other pieces, but this one is a mystery." He glanced up. "Ninon's father had the dagger and pistols assessed but not the apothecary. Likewise, she mentioned the other heirlooms but not this piece."

McGinnis bent over to study the labels on the small drawers. "It's interesting that the heirlooms, all three of them, are rather treacherous, even the apothecary." She looked up at him.

He smiled faintly. "Then, you must recognize the names of the medicines, as I imagined you would."

"I didn't learn about them in med school, but I do know that early remedies, in some instances, proved lethal to the patient." She pointed at the first small drawer. "*Bryonia Alba*, for instance, was used to treat fevers, but it can be toxic if the dose is excessive. And this one, *Ricinus Communis*, has anti-inflammatory properties, but if you were to swallow a half-dozen seeds, you'd be dead. *Colchicum Autumnale*," she tapped the drawer below, "is good for gout, if administered *externally*, but, ingested, well..." She paused. "It's as lethal as arsenic."

"I think we've got more here than we can tackle in an evening, don't you, Doctor?" He retrieved his hat from the rack.

"Yes, and besides all this, there's the John Doe skeleton to get to." She dropped her glasses into the pocket of her coat.

"*John* Doe?" he said.

"The skeleton is male. I can tell you that much."

"What do you say I buy you a drink, Dr. McGinnis, if you don't have plans. It's the least I can do, uh, after asking you to stay late."

"I'd like nothing better than a drink. I'm feeling the need to clear my head."

"As am I, as am I." He held the door as she slipped off her coat, hung it on the rack, and grabbed her purse.

Chapter Nineteen

Thursday, September 24, Happy Hour
Al's Supper Club, near Hembree

Set behind a sprawling pecan grove on Little Smith, hardly a stone's throw from Larkspur Plantation, Al's Supper Club seemed a logical meeting place for Mosey and her friends, all of whom were involved in one way or another in the John Doe case. Two places in one, it sported an upscale seafood restaurant on one side, a popular jazz club on the other, the latter having evolved over time from what was once an old juke joint. The club side was modern and elegant, with glass cabinetry, zinc counter tops, and an abstract of a jazz band that ran the full length of the room. But, here and there, signs of the building's long-ago past peeked through, especially in the bar, where a remnant of the hardwood dance floor, waxed to a sheen, mirrored plexiglass tables, stylish and brand new.

Mosey entered through the side door that led directly to the bar and sat down at the counter. The barista, prepping for happy hour, was setting out glass trays of orange, lemon, and lime slices on the workspace below the counter. Mosey leaned in to smell the citrus, a pleasant offset to the aroma of blackened seafood that wafted in from the kitchen.

"What can I get for you?" the barista said.

"Nothing yet. I'm waiting for my friends."

"You sure?"

"Well, maybe a daiquiri—the one with grapefruit and grenadine?"

"One Hemingway daiquiri coming up."

"And a soda cracker, if you've got any."

"Would a bread stick do?"

"Sure."

Wrapped in the silence of the empty bar, Mosey soon drifted into thought.

"Sold any houses lately?" came a mildly derisive voice.

"You scared me," she said, turning to face Al Bergeron, owner of the club.

He chuckled. "You were a thousand miles away, girly."

"Not so many as you think." She twisted away from Al's imposing figure and back toward the bar.

The barista set a frosty glass and a basket of bread sticks on the counter.

She reached for her handbag, but Al intervened. "If I can't brighten your mood, let me buy you a drink." He lifted his trim brows, as if to say, *Out with it. Tell ole Al what's bugging you.*

"Well, if you must know," she puffed, "looks like I'm stuck with a stigmatized property *again*." She pushed back her drink and propped her arms on the cool surface of the counter. "The Bilyeu estate," she said in a half whisper. "Ninon Bilyeu was stabbed—you heard about *that*. And now they've found human remains in the cistern behind the old overseer's house at Larkspur."

"Hadn't heard," he whispered back. "The murder, yes, but not the other."

"I guess it hasn't made the newspaper, though I could swear I saw that ole Tab Wilson—"

"You could always work for me," he cut in.

"Right," she replied dryly.

"I'm serious. We could use a good singer, and we haven't had a murder here in, let's see…" His grin broke into laughter.

Not quite up to even a half smile, she rolled her eyes, then glanced toward the front entrance.

"Robert coming?" he said.

"They must be held up at the lab, he and Hugh; but they'll be here directly. Nadia and Saffron, too."

"Excuse me a second." He pulled his buzzing cell phone from his pants pocket. "I'll be right back."

Al headed to the dining room, and Mosey settled back into her somber mood. She stared into the frothy drink, then mindlessly moved the glass in little circles over the glossy surface. It wasn't the transfer of the property that was bothering her. It was that mare's nest— what to call it?—yes, *mare's nest* of vaguely related incidents. First, Rafael showed up with that peculiar map of his. When was that? Tuesday last? That's right—first day of fall, first day of dove season. And that same day, Bilyeu called looking for a summer house.

Mosey darlin,' don't you go actin' like somebody dragged you into this mess.

"Good grief, Daddy."

If you hadn't traipsed off to the Bilyeu place. You had no business—

She set her drink down with a thump. "I'll have you know I had a perfectly good reason for going out there, but *somebody* got there ahead of me, that's all. Those remains might have never come to light, no one would have ever been the wiser—"

Steps came again, and she suspended her brief tête-à-tête with her dead father. She glanced at the entrance. It was Nadia's high heels she heard clicking across the floor.

"Hey girl, what you drinking?" Nadia climbed onto the stool next to hers.

"Hemingway daiquiri."

"Looks tasty. What's in it?"

"Have a sip."

Nadia took a taste and crinkled her nose. "A little grapefruity, but not bad." She waved to the barista, who had entered the bar with a bag of ice. "One of these, please." She lifted Mosey's glass, then set it down, but not before taking a second sip. "So, who's coming?"

"The usual," she said with a sigh, "and Saffron's joining us."

She cocked her head at Mosey. "What's the matter?"

"Rafael de Lobos."

"What about him?"

"I can't help but wonder—" She stopped mid-sentence. "By the way, did you find the sales slip for the portrait?"

"It took a while, but yeah."

"So, who?"

"A man by the name of David Morell—ever heard of him?"

"Morell, yeah." Mosey sat up. "He called the office some time ago."

"Really?" Nadia furrowed her brow.

"But he never called back. Huh. Wonder what the connection is."

"Well, there must be *some* connection," Nadia said,

"and the only thing we've got to go on is his rather specific interest in the Bilyeu estate sale."

"Was there an address, phone number—?"

"An address, yes." She pulled up a note on her phone and passed it to Mosey.

"New Orleans, 727 St. Anne," Mosey read, then passed the phone back to Nadia. "Makes sense. Some of the Bilyeus lived in New Orleans, and looks like they still do."

"We had a number, but the phone's disconnected."

"You tried it?"

"I did."

The barista arrived with Nadia's drink.

"What'd you say this is?" she asked Mosey.

"What?"

"This drink—what is it?"

"Sorry, a Hemingway daiquiri." Mosey shook her head. "I can't get Rafael off my mind. I know he's connected with this Bilyeu business."

"I told Olivera about Rafael's being here. I imagine he'll check it out."

"I need to have a chat with that young man," Mosey said. "There's more to this search for a shotgun house by a round pond than he's saying."

"I told you that yesterday." Nadia reached across Mosey for a bread stick.

She passed the basket to her friend. "Yeah, and *yesterday* we had one corpse, not two."

"Two," Nadia said. "Could be two. Or three or—"

"*Three?*"

Nadia's poker face gave away nothing. She seemed unnaturally calm, in fact, more interested in the bread stick she was nibbling than the rising body count. "I was kidding. For Pete's sake, Mosey, lighten up."

Before she could ascertain if Nadia was kidding or not, Saffron arrived.

"Hey, ladies." Saffron sat next to Nadia. "Where're the gents?"

"They'll be here." Mosey studied Saffron's face. She appeared relaxed, but Mosey knew better. She was biting her lip, and any minute she'd start tapping with that ring of hers. "Nadia found the name of the man who bought the portrait. David Morell. It's got to be the same guy who called the office, remember?"

"Could be," Saffron said, "but that was ages ago."

"Well, it couldn't have been *that* long. I've been at Shepherd Realty a year, a little more?"

"I don't suppose anybody's heard from Olivera." Saffron glanced nervously around the room.

"Nope," Mosey said.

Nadia shook her head. "This go-round, seems like I'm the one giving *him* the information."

"Yeah, well," Saffron said, "he's paid to do the work. Might as well do it. I wouldn't be going out of my way—"

"You reckon Robert and Hugh have made any progress?" Nadia said.

"I imagine they'll have a story to tell." Mosey looked across Nadia at Saffron. "I don't suppose you said anything to your family."

"I preferred not to, but I called Momma. I thought I'd better prepare her, just in case."

"You don't really think it's anybody you know," Nadia said.

Saffron, chin propped on her fist, looked thoughtful, then said, "Hate to say it, but it's highly likely."

153

"I don't know why you'd say that," Mosey said. "There're lots of unknowns here. For one, we don't know how long the body's been down there. How old's the house?"

"About a hundred years," she said, "no, more than that. The old main house must've been built in the 1870s, 1880s. I imagine the overseer's house was built not too long after that."

"And it was renovated when?" Nadia said.

Saffron shook her head. "Not sure, but if we knew that—"

"—we'd know a good bit," Nadia said.

"Huh?" Mosey knitted her brow.

"We'd be able to eliminate some suspects," Nadia said.

"How's that?" As usual, Nadia was a step ahead.

"If they'd renovated the house, they would have fixed the broken drains, don't you think?"

"You're saying they'd have uncovered the cistern and found the body?"

"Right, which makes me think that the body was put there *after* the renovation."

Mosey nodded and took a sip of her drink. "Makes sense."

"What makes sense?" It was Robert standing at her elbow, leaning in to give her a kiss.

Hugh, trailing behind Robert, took a seat next to Saffron.

"You've ordered already," Robert said.

"Yeah," Mosey said, "but just a drink. Would you get me another of these?"

"Sure," he said, "and why don't we get a table." After he'd taken Saffron's and Hugh's orders, he moved down the bar, while the others, following Hugh, moved to a large, round table by the window.

"So, what did you find out?" Mosey said to Hugh, who was pulling out chairs.

He paused and tilted his head. "I'm not sure we ought to be talking about this."

"Why not?" Saffron said.

"Because it's a *police* matter."

"What Olivera doesn't know won't hurt him," was Nadia's retort.

"We don't know anything much, not yet."

"You must know something," Saffron insisted.

"I can tell you this much. It won't be all that difficult to identify the body, if he was from around here."

All eyes were on Hugh.

"It was a man, then." Saffron took a seat.

He nodded.

"And?"

"Some personal items we found near the remains may help with the identification—and I said *may*."

"Like what?" Saffron's eyes narrowed.

"A watch, a belt buckle, and a guitar pick."

Robert was back from the bar with a tray of daiquiris and a basket of breadsticks.

"Robert," Hugh lifted a drink off the tray, "you recall Olivera saying anything about confidentiality?"

"No—why?"

"These women are pressing me for information."

Robert passed Saffron and Nadia their drinks. "Looks like the body was there a good long while. We tested a bone sample for bacterial penetration. I'd say we're dealing with remains from the late sixties or early seventies, right, Hugh?"

"Give a year or two." Hugh offered the breadsticks to Saffron.

"So, these personal effects…" Saffron passed the basket to Mosey. "What *were* they exactly?"

"Like I said, a watch, a belt buckle, and a guitar pick. That was it."

"No clothes, shoes?" Saffron said.

Hugh shook his head. "Clothes go quickly. Hard stuff—bones, teeth, hair—sticks around longer."

"My great-uncle Eugene played the guitar," Saffron said.

"I wouldn't get upset just yet," Robert said. "Half of Hembree plays the guitar."

"You wait," Saffron said. "It's Uncle Eugene."

"When did he go missing?" Mosey said.

"About the time of the war, World War II."

"But wait a minute." Nadia tapped Saffron on the hand. "Hugh said the remains are from the sixties or seventies."

"True," Hugh said, "but the time of disappearance and time of death wouldn't, well, have to coincide. If he was from around here, he might have left, then come back."

"Yeah, I see what you mean," Nadia said.

"I don't," Mosey said.

"Maybe he left in the forties, then came back twenty or thirty years later," Hugh said.

"That doesn't make sense," Mosey said. "If he came back, somebody would have seen him."

"Obviously, somebody *did* see him." Hugh sipped his drink.

"Yeah, I guess so." Mosey frowned.

"Any idea how the victim died?" Nadia said.

Robert shook his head. "The remains are at the coroner's lab. We took a sample to get an age on the bones. Eads will have a better idea about cause of death."

"And, of course, if he was murdered, nobody can tell us who did it," Nadia added.

"Doubtful," Robert concurred.

"I wonder who was living in the overseer's house back then," Nadia said. "Anybody know?"

Saffron looked up. "I reckon it was Arnold, Ninon's father."

"If he was living in the house," Nadia said, "he must have had some inkling that a body was in the cistern."

Mosey made a sound of disgust and then added, "A dead body…"

"Not a body for long," Robert added.

Ignoring the reference to decomposition, Mosey said, "Ninon must have been gone by then. He must have been living there by himself." Then, looking at Saffron, she asked, "Was anybody in your family living on the place when Mr. Arnold was still alive?"

"I think my grandparents were sharecropping. But they didn't move into the overseer's house till after he died."

"When was that?" Mosey said.

Saffron shook her head. "No idea."

"So, it could be," Mosey said, "that nobody except Arnold Bilyeu lived there for years after the murder."

"That's right," Saffron nodded. "But you have to wonder why Mr. Arnold would've murdered somebody and thrown the body in the damn cistern."

"Seems unlikely," Robert said.

"If anybody knows anything about it, my money's on Frank Ferguson."

"What makes you say that?"

"Mr. Jake was an only child," Saffron said, "and so was his son Arnold. They depended on Frank to run the place, both of them. Frank knew everything there was to know about growing cotton, and he knew Larkspur like the back of his hand. So, when Mr. Jake died, Mr. Arnold made Frank the overseer, and he stayed the overseer till Mr. Arnold died and his cousin from New Orleans showed up."

"His cousin?" Robert said.

"Emile Bilyeu."

"Well, if Frank knows something, he'd better speak up," Mosey said.

"I don't know." Saffron shook her head. "You don't bite the hand that feeds you."

"But that was *then*," Robert said.

"I'm not sure that *then* and *now* are any different. Whoever ends up with the place will hire him again. You watch." Saffron shook the ice in the bottom of her glass.

"He's a tad old for overseer," Robert said. "I'd think they'd bring in their own people."

"I still need to talk to Rafael," Mosey said, ambling away from the topic at hand and back to what for her was the starting point of it all.

"That's a terrible idea," Robert said. "Let Olivera do his job—he'll figure it out. Think about it, Mosey. What if this Spanish client of yours knows more than he's letting on, a great deal more, and is prepared to—"

"To what?" she cut in. "Stab me?"

"Worse things have happened," Robert replied.

Unsure how to take her husband's remark, she rolled her eyes.

"Mosey," Nadia said, "you have no idea who this

158

man is, what he wants, or what he'll do to get it."

"Then, at the very least, we need to talk to Olivera," she retorted, "and let *him* know what *we* know." She was determined to make her point with someone, and it might as well be the Police Chief.

"That's a much better idea," Robert said calmly. "First thing tomorrow, I'll call in reference to our report and let him know you'd appreciate an interview soon as possible."

"No, that sounds dumb. I'll call him myself." She pulled out her cell phone and, then and there, called the police station.

"Mosey," Nadia said with alarm.

She clicked off and dropped the phone in her purse.

"What?" Nadia said.

"The station's closed. Voice mail picked up."

"First thing tomorrow," Robert repeated. "Now smile and drink your daiquiri." He slid off the stool and, glass in hand, headed to the bar.

Chapter Twenty

Friday, September 25, morning
The Tavernette

Not that Olivera was big on *abolengo*, but, in order
to track down the murderer of the last of the Hembree
Bilyeus, he needed to sort out the victim's provenance—
odd word to use for a human being. But for certain, there
were clues to be found in the backstories of the three
families: the Hembree and New Orleans Bilyeus and the
Spanish Lobos. He wondered how the superior Bilyeus
happened to mix blood with the Lobos, one of whom, at
minimum, was a thief. He also wondered *qué diablos* had
brought this latter-day Lobos, Rafael, across the ocean to
Hembree, Arkansas.

As he walked into the breakfast room at the
Tavernette, it crossed his mind that he'd interviewed as
many people of interest at Hembree's bed and breakfast
as at the police station. Wasn't true, of course, but it
seemed like it of late. He tipped his hat to Ms. Tisdale,
then hung it on the coat rack.

He checked his watch. Nine-thirty. He'd arrived
before the breakfast hour ended, just in time for biscuits
and sausage gravy. Half blind to the paraphernalia
around him—the busts of military men, the scabbards,
pistols, maps, and photographs—he made his way to a
table in the corner. Bright morning light beamed through

the window, and he tugged at the lace curtains to block the glare.

The last of the customers had departed, and Ruby was clearing the tables, gathering up the soiled napkins and cloths and setting out clean ones. "Hey, Ruby, you still on duty?"

"Why, Lieutenant Olivera, I could ask the same of you."

He chuckled and stood to one side while the waitress straightened the tablecloth and covered it with a linen topper.

"That's right," he said. "I guess the two of us ended our day here."

"If you don't mind my asking, who was that pretty little thing you were slinging back shots with?" After she'd placed a gingham napkin at the side of the plate, she looked straight into his eyes.

"Now, Ruby, don't get any ideas. That was business, just business." He sat, unfolded the napkin, and dropped it in his lap. "But, since you obviously haven't met her— and you should—that was the new coroner, Dr. Eads McGinnis."

"Little Eads. My goodness, of course I know her, but I would never have guessed. She's filled out right nice. Old Dr. McGinnis's daughter, my, my."

Olivera responded with a nod and a wink, as Ruby slid a menu under his nose.

"You'd better order quick. They're about to switch over to the lunch prep."

"Bring me a large coffee and biscuits and gravy, please, ma'am." He handed back the menu.

"You don't want no hash browns, eggs, nothin' else?"

"Well, bring me a couple of tomato slices."

She nodded and hurried away toward the kitchen, crossing paths with Mavis Tisdale, who'd entered the breakfast room with a tray of diminutive vases.

Olivera waggled a finger in the air. "Ms. Tisdale."

"Yes, Lieutenant?"

"I need to speak to another one of your guests. I understand Mr. Lobos, Rafael de Lobos, is staying here."

"I saw him in the parlor just a minute ago." She placed a vase of chrysanthemums on the table. "Want me to see if I can catch him?"

"If you wouldn't mind, and, tell you what, here's my card. Ask him to drop by my table, if he can spare a minute."

She set down her tray, rushing away on his errand. Within minutes, Lobos appeared.

"Lieutenant Olivera? Rafael de Lobos." The young man clicked his heels and bowed slightly.

"*Encantado.*" Olivera stood.

"*Igualmente.* I see I'm not the only one who speaks *castellano.*"

"Yes, but I'd have to say I'm a little rusty."

"Rusty?"

Olivera smiled. "Out of practice." He pushed back a chair for his guest. "Please have a seat. Can I ask Ruby to bring you something? A cup of coffee?"

"I've eaten, but I wouldn't mind another coffee." Lobos sat and, gathering his hair into a ponytail, tied it with a band.

"Thanks for seeing me on short notice."

"Not at all, but I'm confused. You need to speak to *me*?"

"I thought, uh, since you're related to the victim in

the case I'm investigating…"

Without questioning how the lieutenant had come by this information, Lobos simply replied, "Yes, I read about that in the newspaper." He then placed his hands, one over the other, on the table.

"She was your distant cousin?"

"There was some relation between our families, the Bilyeus and the Lobos. But I've lived in Spain all my life, and I don't know my American relatives."

"I see, and yet, you are *here* now."

"Yes," he responded without hesitation, "I have been *sent* here, you might say, by my great-grandfather, though he died many years ago."

"*Sent*?" Olivera repeated.

"Yes. He wanted his son to come to Hembree, but he never made it here, nor did his son's son. Finally, it was left to me. Because, you see, when my father dies, I will become Conde de Lobos. I will inherit the estate along with the title—though such things matter little these days."

It seemed that way, judging from his countenance. Something—reserve, likely—had soaked up the slightest trace of self-importance.

"But your family must have thought it mattered."

"Yes, to my parents it does, and that is why I have come. My great-grandfather, Don José—*que en paz descanse*—passed on a map of Hembree to his son, a map he'd drawn from memory. He sketched in the location of a house he'd wanted his son to see."

"And *have* you seen the house?"

"Yes, I have seen it, but I have not been able to do as my great-grandfather wished."

Hispanic himself, Olivera knew his next question

would be thought impolite, but he asked it anyway, prefacing it with a cough. "Which was?"

"If you must know, to find and bring back some valuables that were stolen from my family many years ago."

"Stolen?" He coughed again. "What, if you don't mind my asking?"

"The most valuable possessions the family had. When the King bestowed the title of *conde* on his friend and confidant Jaime de Lobos, he presented him with a gift of two dueling pistols and a dagger from the royal collection. To us, they are worth more than money. You understand, Lieutenant?"

"Yes, of course."

Ruby arrived with the order.

"Ruby, could you bring another coffee please, for Mr. Lobos?"

"I surely will." She glanced at Olivera's guest. "Black, right?"

"Yes, black, please."

"Sure you wouldn't care for something to nibble on?" she tempted.

"No, thank you, just coffee."

She left, and Olivera resumed his questioning. "And your great-grandfather, he thought the items might be in Hembree?" He couldn't fathom how Hembree, of all places, could have appeared in the cross hairs of a Spanish count. He filled his cup to the brim with cream and carefully sipped.

"He knew they were here," he said with certainty. "He came here himself in the 1930s. He saw the dagger, but he was unable to bring the items back to Spain."

Olivera cut off his first bite of biscuit, barely visible

under a dollop of steaming gravy. He chewed and wiped his mouth with his napkin. "Why was that? I mean, why wasn't he able to get them back? Did he seek the help of the law?"

"No, he believed the law wouldn't be willing to help him, because the man who possessed the weapons was very powerful, and he and Don José were enemies."

Olivera frowned.

"They were enemies," Lobos repeated. "They were distantly related, but they were enemies."

"Who *was* this man, the enemy of your great-grandfather?" Olivera squirmed in his chair.

"Mr. Jake Bilyeu. Bilyeu's grandmother was my relative. Her name was Fernanda de Lobos. But I must add, Lieutenant, that she was not a family member we are proud of." He lowered his eyes.

"Indeed," he said, noting that Lobos's reference to his long-deceased something-or-other had churned up genuine discomfort.

Ruby arrived with a cup for Lobos and a pot of fresh coffee. She served the lieutenant first, then his guest. "The kitchen's closed for breakfast, but I could get you a donut, if you want."

"No, just the coffee," Lobos responded with a smile.

"Suit yourself," Ruby said.

Lobos stirred his coffee and continued. "Fernanda de Lobos has nothing to do with my being here, and I would prefer to let sleeping dogs lie—I believe you say that."

Olivera nodded. "Yes, that's right—sleeping dogs lie. Your English is very good, by the way."

Lobos sipped his coffee and, without any coaxing, returned to the subject at hand. "So, Don José returned

165

to Spain. He would have come back here at a later date, but he was killed some few years later, in the war, the Spanish Civil War."

"Hmm." He folded his hands and thought. "It fell to you, then, to do what your great-grandfather would have done had he lived."

"Yes, that's right."

"To come here, approach the current owner of the estate, Ninon Bilyeu—"

"No, that was not my intention. I wanted to find the weapons myself, where they were hidden, and take them." He paused. "I am not proud of that, but you must understand that these things are my father's. They belong to *him*, not the Bilyeus."

"You must have gone to the hermitage—the small cottage where Ninon was living."

"No, I went to the house near the old house, now in ruins. *That* is where Don José saw the heirlooms...well, only the dagger. He saw Mr. Jake Bilyeu, in a rage, remove the dagger from its hiding place."

"The dagger was hidden, you say."

"Jake Bilyeu had very cleverly made a place for it, inside the wooden frame of the front door."

"I can tell you for certain that it isn't there now. The dagger and the pistols were in a trunk, buried in Ninon's garden, which is nowhere near the plantation."

"I thought they might be where Don José had seen them. I didn't know where else to look." Lobos sipped again, set down his cup, and leaned forward. "But then a man came, a priest, and I hid behind the house. He walked around the side of the house and stopped at a—I don't know how to call it."

"A big cover, over a hole?" Olivera said.

He nodded. "Yes, some kind of cover. He pushed it to one side."

"Go on."

"He bent down to look but stopped, like maybe he heard something. Then he left. As soon as he was gone, I tried to open the doors, but they were locked. So, I tried the windows, but they were locked, too. Then I noticed a broken window. I reached in and unlocked it, but I couldn't raise it. It was stuck."

Olivera took another bite of biscuit, wiped his mouth, and placed his fork and knife on his plate. Staring directly into Lobos's hazel eyes, he said, "So you never spoke to Sister Clare, never went to the hermitage?"

"No, I did not. I learned she'd been murdered, and I hesitated to go back to Larkspur. I wasn't sure what to do, since it was now a crime scene. I read about it in the paper, as I said before."

"Yes, because as you know, skeletal remains were found on the property. That was a *cistern* you saw the priest uncover."

"Cistern, like *cisterna*?"

"The same."

"Why, I wonder?"

"I can only guess," Olivera said. "But more to the point, I need to know who this priest was. Did you get a good look at him?"

"He was about ten, fifteen meters away."

"His coloring, age, anything?"

"Coloring?"

"What color was his hair, his complexion?"

"Very light skin, light hair."

"And you say he pushed the cover aside to look in—anything else?"

"I think he didn't want to be seen. He left quickly."

"Did you look in the cistern?"

"No, I didn't. I needed to get *inside* the house. As I said before, I tried to open the door, then a window, but I couldn't get in, so I left."

"What time of day did all this happen?"

"After lunchtime, maybe one, one thirty?"

"So definitely before two?"

"I'm not sure. Does it matter?"

"It could matter a great deal. Sister Clare was killed around two-thirty, three."

"I'm sorry, Lieutenant, but I wasn't paying close attention to the time."

"You know that Sister Clare was stabbed." He pushed his plate aside and, folding his napkin, placed it on the table.

"Yes, I read that."

"I strongly suspect the dagger you were looking for *is* the murder weapon."

Lobos's only response was a frown.

"The heirlooms were buried in her garden next to the cottage. We found something else buried with the dagger and pistols—maybe another heirloom. A small apothecary, *una pequeña botica*, inside a book." He paused. "You know anything about that?"

"I have never heard of any *botica*—what did you call it?"

"Apothecary, where medicinal herbs were kept. But this is a very old item, like a book with small drawers inside. Whatever you might know would be helpful."

"Medicines," Lobos repeated, followed by a heavy sigh. "Yes, I think I know something," he said, almost in a whisper, the color drained from his face.

The young man, forthright until then, had come to an impasse, apparently. He glanced away before looking back and saying in a grave voice, "Honor—*el qué dirán*—matters a great deal to us."

Though American-born, Olivera had heard plenty about *honra, honor,* and *el qué dirán* from his Mexican-born parents and grandparents, though he'd never been able to sort them out exactly. "Yes, honor, I understand," was the best he could do.

"Maybe you *do* understand. Your name is Olivera." Lobos leaned forward. "That *botica*, apothecary as you called it, belonged to Fernanda de Lobos and her husband. They committed a...*crimen horible*."

Olivera couldn't fathom why Lobos had suddenly switched to Spanish. *Crimen horible*, horrible crime. They sounded about the same.

Before continuing with his revelation, Lobos looked away again, this time in sorrow. "They killed people, slaves."

Olivera's eyes narrowed. "Go on."

"Fernanda de Lobos, she married a *farmaceútico*—how do you say?"

"Pharmacist."

"Yes, pharmacist," he repeated. "She married a pharmacist. His name was Hershel Bilyeu. They opened a store, one of the first pharmacies in New Orleans. He hired a Haitian priestess who'd come to New Orleans after the slave rebellion. She had knowledge of herbs and potions. He and the woman used his house slaves as *conejillos de Indias*—how do you say?"

"Guinea pigs."

"Yes, guinea pigs. They tested their medicines on Bilyeu's slaves. The slaves died, all of them, and Bilyeu and his wife left New Orleans right away. The priestess, she was arrested and hanged."

Olivera's brows lifted. "And how did you come by this information?"

"Is it not enough, Lieutenant, that I have told you these things?"

"Well…," he stammered, then scratched his temple. Was there a reason, an important one, to press Lobos on his source? Unable to think of one, with a motion of his hand, he encouraged him to continue.

"Before they left, Fernanda went to her father's house and took the valuable heirlooms her father had stolen from *his* father. He'd taken them to Louisiana from Spain. A most dishonorable thing for a son to do."

"Yes," he said, "dishonorable, quite." Attempting to offer a restorative word, he said, "But you and your family weren't involved in any of this, correct?"

"My family does not wish to be involved in any way with these Lobos or Bilyeus." He rapped his knuckles lightly on the table. "You could say that I am an heir to this land, this Larkspur. But it belonged to people who dishonored our name." He paused and then said, "All this will come out?"

Olivera briefly considered his obligation before saying, "I'm afraid so. I must contact the New Orleans authorities and let them know. I really must."

Lobos sat for a moment, his face engulfed in apprehension. "This will be in the newspapers."

The sun's glare had diminished to a shimmer, and Olivera was able to look out at the sidewalk, where people were gathering for the farmers market. He had no doubt now that Rafael de Lobos had come to Hembree on a mission of honor. He was pretty sure he wouldn't have killed to reclaim the heirlooms. Apparently, he wouldn't have even broken down the door of the house where he suspected they were hidden. On the other hand, would he have killed to protect the family honor? Maybe he *had* gone to the hermitage. Maybe he *had* killed Ninon, not for the heirlooms buried in her garden, but to prevent her from revealing something about the family. But what? How much of her family history had the Poor Clare known?

He looked back at Lobos, wanting not to ask any more questions, wanting, instead, to console the young man who sat across from him in despair. But that wasn't his job, was it? He took a deep breath and spoke honestly. "I can't tell you exactly what they will do with this information—if not the newspapers, maybe the history books, or some exhibit at the New Orleans Apothecary Museum, which is where, I imagine, this book of medicines or poisons will end up." He rose from his chair, picking up Lobos's ticket and his own, which Ruby had quietly placed on the table. "I'll get this."

Lobos thanked him and stood. "Lieutenant Olivera, I am sorry that I did not speak to you before now."

"Well, I understand your situation, but maybe you should speak with Ms. Frye." He felt generous of a sudden, even where Mosey Frye was concerned. "You know you got her involved in this."

"Yes, of course."

"You won't be leaving right away, I assume."

"Soon, Lieutenant, but not right away."

Olivera placed a couple of bills on the table. He took a step toward the entrance but then paused. He should probably ask Lobos to stop by the station for prints. But, no, he could spare him the public humiliation. "Please get in touch before you leave."

Lobos nodded and bent slightly at the waist before exiting the breakfast room a few steps behind Olivera.

Chapter Twenty-One

Friday, September 26, mid-morning
Hembree Square

Olivera's cellphone rang as he was leaving the Tavernette. "Robert, I've been hoping to hear from you." Quickening his step, he made his way through the crowd of shoppers to a stone bench tucked under the broad canopy of a live oak.

"I just now emailed you the report," Robert said, "you and Eads."

"Good." He perched on the edge of the bench. "I'll have a look as soon as I get to the station." He took off his straw hat and fanned his face.

"The victim was male, and if I had to say how long he'd been down there, I'd say since the late 1960s, early 1970s."

"Well, that's a start. Thanks for your work on this, you and Hugh both."

"We found a few items that may help with the identification."

"Like what?"

"A watch, a buckle, and a guitar pick."

"That's it?"

"Afraid so. By the way, if you wouldn't mind giving Mosey a call."

"Sure," he answered without hesitation. "What's

up?" Robert had willingly helped with the excavation—how could he not repay the favor?

"She has some information to pass along…about Rafael de Lobos."

"I've just spoken with Lobos."

"She says it's important, so if you wouldn't mind…"

"Of course, no problem." Huh. Anything Mosey-related was a problem or, if not, an annoyance in the very least. He mentally shuffled the promised call to the bottom of the stack and slipped his cell into his pocket.

Getting to his car, he rolled down the windows and sat pondering. Should he stop by the police station or head to Conakry? A second interview with Mannix couldn't be put off. He had to have known about the body in the cistern. Why else would he have gone there? Since their meeting at St. Patrick's, he'd suspected him of something, though he wasn't sure what. The scene loomed in his mind. The austere façade of the church, the dark sanctuary, the monsignor's meagerly furnished cubby hole—all absurdly gothic, like the set of an old horror film. He pressed the ignition button and pulled away from the curb.

Certain that Mannix knew about the John Doe murder, he couldn't imagine why he'd returned to the crime scene. The priest's mere presence, regardless of his reason, strongly implied he knew what he would find. Before confronting him, however, he wanted to speak to McGinnis, learn all he could about John Doe's demise.

He turned off Lexington onto Old Goshen Road. The sooner he got to Conakry, the better. He decided not to call—a call would tip him off. He'd take his chances on catching him at the church.

He rang the coroner's office. "Dr. McGinnis, sorry

to bother you."

"No bother. What's up?"

"You're at the lab?"

"Where else on a Friday morning?"

"Right. I've just heard from Robert Ellison, and he gave me an estimated time of death."

"I've got the report in front of me."

"Any notion of cause?"

"Knife wound, I'm thinking, but don't hold me to it."

He sighed. "Another stabbing."

"Looks like."

"Ellison says they found some things that might help with the identification."

"I've got them right here."

"Okay, so let's do this. Check the records and see what you can come up with. Any teeth?"

"A full set."

"Good," he said, "and I'll start putting a list together of people who lived or worked at Larkspur. Maybe Carlotta Humphrey can pull a few names out of that big file of hers."

"I'll get started on it, Lieutenant. Anything else?"

"No, I'll let you get back to work. I'll be in touch."

It was eleven or a little after when he arrived at St. Patrick's and pulled up alongside the monsignor's sedan. He got out and headed into the sanctuary, which was a little brighter than the last time he was there. Sunlight streamed through the tiny windows in the side walls, setting the crucifix ablaze. Quite a lovely sight, actually, despite the somberness of the surroundings. "Good morning," he called out to a woman kneeling at the railing, not praying but cleaning the steps that led to the altar.

She raised her head and turned in his direction. "Good morning."

"I'm looking for Monsignor Mannix. Don't suppose you've seen him."

"He was here a little while ago."

"You wouldn't happen to know where he is now?"

"Well, he might be in his office. I can show you." She set her scrub brush on a step and started to get up.

"That's okay, ma'am. I know the way."

He walked around the side of the church to the monsignor's office and knocked.

He opened right away. "Lieutenant Olivera, I wasn't expecting to see *you* again. I was finishing my homily for five-o'clock mass."

"I won't take much of your time." He peered into the uninviting space. If not for the heat, he'd as soon remained at the doorstep.

"I've already told you everything I know. I can't imagine—"

"Well," Olivera interrupted, "not, uh, *everything*."

"I don't know what you mean."

"I won't beat about the bush, Monsignor. Turns out you were seen at Larkspur Plantation last Tuesday, the day Sister Clare was murdered. Someone saw you push aside the platform that covers the cistern at the back of the overseer's house." He scrutinized the priest's face as he conveyed the final jolt. "Which, by the way, is where we've just discovered the skeletal remains of a person, a man, actually."

Mannix shoved the pen he'd been twisting in his hands into his pocket. "And this witness, this person who claims to have seen me?" He stepped inside, motioning for him to follow.

"You're suggesting he was mistaken?"

"No, but sometimes people misinterpret."

"Witnesses do misinterpret, and that's why I'm here, to find out what you can tell me about your whereabouts on Tuesday, September 22."

"If I could speak on my behalf, I willingly would tell you what I know, but you see—"

"So, you were there on someone else's behalf, a confessant perhaps?"

"My first concern is for the faithful, and when they entrust me with a confidence…" He stood beside his desk, looking down at his homily.

"Two people are dead, Monsignor. If these deaths are related in any way, if Sister Clare, for example, was silenced by the person who killed the other victim, you need to tell me what you know."

"Sister Clare and I, we've…" He broke off mid-sentence and slumped onto the bench. As if speaking to some invisible presence, he said in a faint voice, "My duty here is not clear to me."

"Monsignor, if there's anything you can reveal, without breaking the Seal of Confession, please do." He sat in the armchair, removed his hat, and slowly turned it in his hands. "Anything you feel you can tell me…"

"I've lived with this for a long time, and now that Sister Clare is dead, I suppose it doesn't matter. It isn't her confession I've been protecting." He lifted his eyes. "It's the confession of her father."

Whatever it was Olivera thought he had seen in the monsignor's face was no longer there. The man was expressionless, every bit as drab as his surroundings, as if, in forsaking his promise, he'd abandoned his sacred

177

vocation. He shifted in his chair. "Arnold Bilyeu, you mean. But he wouldn't have confessed to you. You weren't even here then."

"Not to me."

"To your predecessor, then, or Father Moody?"

He shook his head. "To his daughter, before he died. I respected the promise she'd given a penitent close to death." He rose and stood at the window that looked out on a grove of cottonwoods. "I'll tell you what I know, but I *do not know* who killed Sister Clare."

Under other circumstances, he would have pulled out his tablet or a recorder. This time, he did not. He sat and listened as the distraught priest began.

"I met Sister Clare when she was a young nun at a small convent near Memphis. She'd just returned from burying her father. It was the first time we'd spoken of anything of a personal nature. She wasn't able to grieve because of her father's disturbing confession. She told me he'd been involved in a murder. She wasn't sure if he or someone else—someone who worked on his place, she thought—had taken the man's life."

He broke in. "Did she know who the victim was or why he'd been murdered?"

"If she knew, she didn't say, and I didn't press her to reveal more. She'd promised her father to keep his secret."

"What about the circumstances? Did she give any indication...?"

"Her father—Arnold Bilyeu was his name—thought the man had come to rob him. There was a struggle. Her father, or maybe the other man, she didn't say—"

"Who *was* the other man?"

"She claimed not to know, and I had no reason not

to believe her. But over time, she began to suspect who that person might be."

"It never occurred to her—or to you—to contact the police?"

"It was a terrible struggle for her. She prayed about it incessantly."

"But the victim's family."

"Yes, of course, but she knew very little, except that he'd attempted to rob her father, or maybe he hadn't. She wasn't at all clear about that."

"The day you went to the house, you must have had a pretty good idea what you would find."

"I wasn't sure *what* I would find."

"Then, why did you go?"

"On Sister Clare's behalf. She had begun to make plans. She wanted her family's land to be a functioning farm again. Her cousin from New Orleans was coming that day. She had suspected all along that her father and his accomplice had hidden the body. She feared the victim hadn't had a proper burial and asked me to drive out to Larkspur, look around the property. Something had stuck in her memory about the cistern near the overseer's house, which is where her father was living when he died. The main house had gone to rack and ruin. Her father didn't have the money to keep it up. When she was a child, during the dry months, they'd pumped water from the cistern to water the garden. But some years later her father, with no explanation, had had it dismantled."

"Her father told her about the murder, and that was it? Didn't tell her who or what he'd done with the body?"

"Did you know Sister Clare?" Mannix said.

"No, sorry to say I never met her."

"She was a very special person, almost childlike. To

have told her anything so ghastly would have been very difficult, I'm sure. My guess is her father couldn't bring himself to say any more than he'd said."

Childlike... He wished Mannix had kept that to himself. "So, after you checked the cistern," he cleared his throat, "I suppose you drove to the hermitage."

"No. I thought I'd been seen. I left quickly, without completing my mission."

"So, you didn't see the remains?"

"No, nothing."

"Did you see Sister Clare after that?"

"No." Mannix placed his hands over his eyes. "I never got to tell her anything."

He wasn't sure if he felt relief or consternation. He had a better picture of the situation, but no better idea of who killed Sister Clare. The man in the cistern, on the other hand, had almost certainly met his demise at the hands of her father or someone on the place. As for Mannix, his explanation was believable. He could no longer consider him a suspect. As much as he hated to admit it, it was a bit of a letdown. He'd been suspicious of the priest's involvement in the death of his confessant.

Olivera cleared his throat again. "Well, I suppose, inadvertently, you and Rafael de Lobos have supplied each other with alibis. Looks like both of you were at Larkspur around the time of Sister Clare's murder."

Mannix's eyes flicked from the window to Olivera. "I don't understand."

"When we spoke before, I mentioned that heirlooms had been found buried in Sister Clare's garden."

Mannix returned to his bench. "Yes, I remember."

"According to Mr. Lobos, who arrived in Hembree this week, a distant relative of his, Fernanda de Lobos,

Hershel Bilyeu's wife, had them in her possession. They settled here about the time of the Civil War. By all appearances, she stole them from her father, and they were passed down secretly from one generation to the next. Sister Clare was the first to mention them in her will. The man who saw you at the house was there hoping to reclaim the Lobos heirlooms."

"So, you thought the motive was related to her wealth?"

He nodded. "I thought that whoever killed Sister Clare might have done so for her sizeable estate: Larkspur, the heirlooms... But now I'm thinking it was this other business, the other murder, committed by her father or someone who worked for him. If that's so, I have to find this individual as soon as possible."

"You're saying if he killed Sister Clare, he might kill again...to protect himself?"

He nodded. "Looks like Sister Clare died because of what she knew." He stood to go but looked back at Mannix. "Let's suppose the killer thinks that *you* know, or Father Moody."

"What are you suggesting, Lieutenant?"

"I need to speak to Father Moody right away, send a couple of men out to the church. But the perpetrator is just as likely to target you, since you were her confessor. I'll get someone over here from the local force."

"I can look out for myself. I wouldn't want to alarm the parishioners."

"The parishioners would prefer to be alarmed than to see you dead."

"I'll be careful. After mass, I'll drive to Mound City. I have friends there."

"I cannot overstress the danger."

Mannix nodded and opened the door.

He turned back. "I don't suppose you've had any strange phone calls?"

Mannix shook his head.

"Anyone hanging around the church?"

"No, no one I'm aware of."

"Don't hesitate to call me, Monsignor. You have my card, right?"

"Yes, and Lieutenant, thank you."

"One more thing. You don't happen to know exactly when you were at Larkspur, do you? Mr. Lobos was a little vague on the time."

"I think it was maybe one-thirty. I'm pretty sure I'd left by two or so. I didn't park right at the house. I walked over from the cemetery. Must have taken ten minutes, more or less."

"Well, that pretty much matches up with what Lobos said. Thanks, Monsignor, and don't take any chances, okay?"

Chapter Twenty-Two

Friday, September 26, noon
Morgue, Delta Infirmary

Olivera sauntered along the dimly lit hall of Delta Infirmary, then stopped at the door to the morgue. About to knock, instead, he stood looking at the plaster walls on either side of the door. Faded and cracked, they intimated a more prosperous time when the local gentry had built themselves a hospital as comfortable and stylish as their parlors. The curved arches and terrazzo floors reminded him of buildings he'd grown up around in California. But it wasn't nostalgia that caused him to linger. It was the coroner herself. They'd been out drinking the night before, and he was feeling a little awkward, feared it might show plainly on his face. He glanced up at the transom over the door. The light was on, so she must be in—poking around, no doubt, in some smelly thing or another. He shoved the door and took out a handkerchief in case he needed to cover his nose.

"Dr. McGinnis," he said, though he'd called her by her given name the night before, "glad you're here."

"Good morning, Lieutenant." She flashed a smile.

"And how's that coming?"

She moved from the gurney to the counter and, in doing so, exposed the remains of the man who, some forty years before, had been stabbed and dumped in a cistern. "Well, I'd say." She positioned something small under a magnifying glass and beckoned. "Take a look at this. It'll help us identify the deceased."

He put his handkerchief back in his pocket and looked at the object, which was a strand of hair, then glanced again at the gurney.

"John Doe was African American."

"Have you determined his age?"

"Over fifty, sixty at most."

"And height?"

"Six feet, more or less."

"Looks like we've got a good bit to go on. And the personal effects?"

She directed his attention to a white cloth on the counter, where the victim's belongings were displayed. She picked up an oval piece of metal. "This buckle is rather distinctive, wouldn't you say?" She pointed to what was left of an engraving.

"What's this?"

"A treble clef, plain as day."

"If you say so."

"John Doe might have been a musician."

"Uh-*huh*," he said, though not entirely convinced.

"If he'd been a laborer, you'd expect to find more degeneration." She stepped to the gurney. "These aren't the knees and ankles of a farm or factory worker. And look at the hands. Not a sign of arthritis."

He glanced at the skeleton and nodded, then shifted his attention to the items on the counter. "Any clues from the watch?"

She held the silver pocket watch to the light that emanated from under the metal cabinetry. "You can still make out an initial or part of an initial on the front of the case. What do you think it is?"

"Hmm. Could be an R or a B."

"Or a D."

"We could save ourselves some time by checking with someone who was around back then."

"And had contacts in the Black community. I wasn't born yet, but I can think of several people who were."

"Like?"

She switched off the light and walked toward her desk. "Evelyn McCutter or Father Moody." She sat in the swivel chair and plunked her readers down on a stack of folders. "How old is Father Moody, you think?"

He shrugged. "Sixtyish?" He pulled his tablet and pencil from his breast pocket and made a note. "So, Moody, Evelyn McCutter..." He stopped writing. "And we can assume the deceased was known to the Bilyeus, given the murder most probably occurred on their land."

McGinnis tilted her head. "Well, in that regard, the evidence isn't telling us much, is it?"

"I guess not," he said. "He might have been killed somewhere else, then the body transported—"

"Regardless of *where* he was killed," she intervened, "we can safely assume that whoever killed him either lived or worked there. It's unlikely a complete stranger would have known about the cistern."

"That's a safe assumption." Good, he thought, she was thinking beyond the evidence. "We've seen the end of the Hembree Bilyeu line, looks like, but some of their laborers are still around. Frank Sr. worked at Larkspur a good while. If John Doe was associated with the place, I imagine he would've known him."

She leaned back in her chair. "What about Carlotta Humphrey? She has the plantation records, doesn't she?"

"True," he nodded, "and, anyway, I need to speak to her." He slipped the tablet and pencil in his pocket. "I'll call her, see what she can come up with."

"I'll contact the county health clinic, ask them about medical records." She cleaned her readers on the hem of her lab coat and slid them on.

"Yes, please do." He glanced toward the skeleton. "Any fractures, anything that might show up on an x-ray?"

"No sign of a broken bone, nothing unusual, except for the nick on the rib. The skeletal structure is in good shape otherwise, considering the deceased's age." She returned to the gurney, slipped on gloves, and picked up the rib bone in question.

He stepped to her side. "Any similarity between the two lesions—this one and the one on Ninon's spine?"

"Un-huh," she nodded, "could've been made by the same weapon."

"Interesting." He rubbed his cheek. "I think I'll give Carlotta a call." He began to pace. "And if you could check the county medical records—"

"—and we can pray, Lieutenant, that the deceased was from around here, because if he wasn't..."

"I'll check the missing persons reports from the sixties and seventies." He glanced at his watch. "Before I go, I wanted to pass along what I learned this morning about the apothecary." He approached the counter where the antique book had lain. "Where'd it go?"

She pulled out a long, deep drawer at the bottom of the counter. "I put the heirlooms in here for safe keeping. Shall we have a look?"

He peeked in and saw that the dagger and pistols were there as well. "Yes, but just the apothecary."

She opened the book and set it upright on the counter.

He bent down and read the labels. "You included the names of the items in the little drawers in your report?"

"I did."

"By the way," he said, looking up. "As it turns out, a distant cousin of Sister Clare's—Rafael de Lobos is his name—"

"Yes," she said with anticipation."

"He's here."

"In Hembree?"

"And get this. He came here precisely, *precisely*, I say"—he drummed his fingertips on the counter—"to recover the heirlooms we dug up."

Frowning in disbelief, she stared at him over the top of her readers.

"I know," he said. "Far-fetched but true. Got it from the horse's mouth this morning. His great-grandfather was here in the twenties, and he and Jake Bilyeu, Ninon's grandfather, were enemies. For whatever reason, they got into a squabble at the overseer's cottage, and Bilyeu pulled a dagger, *that* dagger there, out of the doorframe and threatened him."

"Doorframe," she repeated. "The dagger was hidden in a doorframe?"

"Bizarre, but that's what he said. So, Rafael," he continued, "went to Larkspur Tuesday around midday, thinking he'd get into the house and find the dagger, still hidden, or so he thought, in the doorframe. But, in the meantime, guess who shows up?"

"I haven't the slightest."

"Monsignor Mannix."

"From Conakry?"

"The same. But Rafael, seeing Mannix arrive, ducked behind the house and watched as he lifted the platform, the one over the cistern."

"Lieutenant—" Her eyebrows went up.

He threw his hands out in front of him. "Hold on, let me finish. So, Mannix knew exactly what he would find. Well, maybe not *exactly,* but he suspected, actually, it was Ninon who suspected that a body had been hidden there years before, and she sent Mannix to look for it."

"*How* did she suspect?"

"Her father confessed on his death bed—get this— his involvement in a murder."

She gaped. "You mean *this* murder? The murder of John Doe?"

"*This* murder."

"How very unusual." Her response came almost in a whisper, as her eyes wandered uneasily from the bones to the items on the counter and from the counter to the drawer where the dagger and pistols were stowed. "We know the murderer, but not the victim. The murderer but *not* the person he killed."

"Well, maybe the murderer, maybe one of the murderers. And we can guess the murder weapon."

"The dagger, of course," she mumbled, her eyes widening.

"And not only that, we've got a possible motive for the crime."

She turned toward him. "You're saying, then, that someone killed Sister Clare because she knew—"

"—about this other murder"—he gestured toward the skeleton—"and, apparently, was on the verge—"

"—of what? Telling?"

"Exactly." He wasn't especially fond of having his

188

sentences completed but when she did it, he didn't mind so much.

"Uh-huh." She rubbed her right temple, staring out at nothing in particular. He'd seen her do that before when running something over in her mind. "But wait a second," she said, "how do you know that?"

"Easy." He shrugged. "Mannix fessed up. I had to check out Rafael's story, so, I left the Tavernette and drove to Conakry—again—thinking he was involved in Sister Clare's murder."

"All *this*—" She stopped.

"Apparently, none of it had anything to do with the perpetrator's motive. Mannix said Bilyeu didn't confess to the murder. He confessed to his *involvement* in the murder. So, whoever else was involved—"

"—killed Ninon."

She'd put it together, followed his every mental trail, and agreed with his conclusions.

Her eyes came to rest on the victim's bones. "The man who killed John Doe killed Ninon to keep her from telling." She looked up at Olivera. "And who might that be, Lieutenant?"

"I don't know. But someone close to Arnold—had to have been. A friend or a family member or somebody who worked for him. Which is another reason, come to think of it, I need to speak to Carlotta. The names of the perpetrator and the victim are somewhere in that big file of hers. I don't know how much she's got or how far back the records go, but I know the wills go back several generations."

"And what about the apothecary? What else did Rafael say?"

"That's another can of worms entirely, if what he

told me is on the level. He knows the Lobos family history going *way* back, even before their arrival in Louisiana. His great-great-something or other was Fernanda de Lobos, the wife of the first Hembree Bilyeu. They came here running from the law. Hershel, her husband, was a pharmacist and was working with a Haitian priestess—"

"Haitian priestess?" Her chin lifted. "How much more *exotic* can this whole business get?"

"That's what he said, a Haitian priestess. They concocted some medicines and tested them on his house slaves. They all died, and Hershel and his wife took off, leaving the Haitian woman to take the fall."

"So, the apothecary," she said as she gestured toward the still open book, "once belonged to Hershel Bilyeu, and, for all intents and purposes, is yet *another murder weapon*?"

"That's right. The dagger and pistols belonged to his wife and the apothecary, to him."

"This is most remarkable." She stood and walked toward the counter.

"I'll tell you what my professor used to say, and I've learned he was absolutely right. Crimes crop up again and again. You think you've finished with a case—"

"Like the Princess Paulownia tree," she cut in. She closed the book distractedly and returned it to the drawer.

"Princess what?" he asked with a tilt of his head.

"There was this tree or maybe it was a weed—I was never sure. It came up year after year, no matter how often Daddy chopped it down. He'd hack it down to the ground on one side of the porch, and it'd pop up on the other. The roots just wouldn't let go."

"That was exactly my professor's point. In families,

predispositions of the darkest kind recede, then surface again. That's just the way he said it, *recede, then surface again*. You'd never think, and then suddenly…" He paced away from the counter and, rounding the gurney, came to a stop in the center of the room. "Dr. McGinnis, you realize that if not for the murder of the last remaining Bilyeu—"

"—who was an innocent."

"A sacrificial lamb, just trying to set things right."

"Very sad." She locked the drawer and slipped the key into her pocket of her lab coat.

"Well, I'd like to finish the job," he said.

"By finding the murderer of John Doe?"

He nodded.

"I wonder if the perpetrator is still alive." She stood before the skeleton, looking not at the hands or the ribs where dagger had met bone, but at the skull, the hollow cavities where eyes had once been.

"It's been forty years." He looked at the skull. "Let's say the accomplice was thirty. He'd be seventy now."

"Even if he is alive, he could be long gone from Hembree. The chance of finding DNA evidence on a skeleton… Too much time has passed. There's nothing left that could've carried a print or DNA. The only physical evidence we've got suggestive of a crime is the lesion on the rib."

"I'll speak to Carlotta, see if she can come up with anything that could point to the accomplice."

"Sister Clare didn't know?"

"Mannix said she was vague on the subject. Didn't seem to know who the accomplice was *or* the victim. And she only suspected the body might be in the cistern because her father had disconnected the drain."

"But you think whoever killed Ninon did it to keep her from revealing her father's secret?"

"That's my theory."

"It's all kind of creepy, like that dagger."

"What?"

"It's as if it had a life of its own."

"Nadia Abboud says it belonged to a Spanish king, Carlos II, the one who was called *El Hechizado*—the Cursed."

She glanced down again. "He wasn't the only one."

"Looks like."

Chapter Twenty-Three

Friday, September 25, afternoon
Hembree Town Square

On his way to the town square, Olivera went over
the notes in his tablet. From the beginning of the
investigation, he'd jotted down every guarded remark,
every expression or tone suggestive of something being
amiss. On close inspection, none of his people of interest
seemed more suspicious than the others. Initially, he was
ready to pin the murder—Sister Clare's—on one of the
priests or somebody with a grudge, a disgruntled relative,
for example. But once he'd seen the will, it became clear
that she'd treated her potential heirs fairly, with one
exception—Lobos, whom, apparently, she'd never met.
But after speaking with the man, he was pretty sure he
wasn't a killer. Besides that, Lobos had a firm alibi for
the time of the murder, as did Mannix.

He crossed off Mannix. Then the cousins—Bilyeu,
DeGroat, and Lobos. That left Moody and the Fergusons.
Opportunity? Probably. But motive? Nothing, nothing
he could fathom, might have prompted a Ferguson to kill
Sister Clare. If she'd lived to amend her will, how might
they or any of them, for that matter, have been affected?
Nothing really significant came to mind. The church, of
course, would have lost the heirlooms, just as Blanchard
would have lost the old buildings. He wondered what the

buildings themselves, such as they were, might be worth as historical artifacts. The Fergusons didn't figure in any of it, as far as he could see. He didn't have anything on them, not a thing, unless...

He arrived at Frye, Frye, and Humphrey and tried the knob, but as half expected, it was locked. His eyes scanned the square. The crowd of Hembreeites who'd been there earlier had shrunk to a handful of dawdlers. The farmers market was closing, and the stall attendants were loading their left-over produce onto trucks. He tucked his tablet in his pocket and continued along the sidewalk, coming to a halt at the back of an old two-tone pickup. He recognized the man lifting a box of tomatoes onto the truck bed. He picked a tomato out of a basket. "You know, Frank, we're heading into October, and it's still hot as blazes. You plant any pumpkins this year?"

Ferguson, in neatly ironed overalls and a trim straw hat, set his box down. "You thinkin' about Halloween already?" He removed his hat and extended a knobby hand.

"How's it going, Frank?" Olivera said as he shook Frank's hand.

"Not bad, Lieutenant, considering." He wiped his brow with the sleeve of his gingham shirt.

"Before you haul those off, how about filling a sack with your ripest tomatoes. Think I'll make a bowl of cool gazpacho."

"Go ahead and grab the ones you want." He handed him a paper bag. "But I wouldn't have figured you for a cook." He chuckled.

"No cooking to it. Just throw a few vegetables into a food processor and—"

Before he could finish enlightening Frank Sr. on the

particulars of a good California-style gazpacho, Frank Jr., who was sitting in the cab, rolled the window down and shouted, "Daddy!"

"Hold on, son. I was helping the lieutenant here."

Frank Jr. opened the door and stepped out. "Sorry, Lieutenant, didn't see you."

"Looks like you've raised a fine crop of tomatoes, Frank. Can't make a good gazpacho without ripe, tasty tomatoes."

Frank Jr. sniggered. "That's like tomato soup, right? Except people eat it cold."

"Uh-huh, you ever try it?"

"No, can't say I have."

"Think I'll take a couple of green peppers, too."

"Pardon me for, uh, bringing it up," Frank Sr. cut in, "but I was wondering. You got any idea who killed Sister Clare?"

Olivera frowned. "Afraid not, but we may be getting close. I don't suppose either of you has remembered anything."

"Nope, not a thing," Frank Jr. said, "but it sure was strange, finding—"

"Finding her dead like that?" He dropped a pepper in his sack.

The older Ferguson lowered his eyes. "Well, yeah, and finding that, uh, *skeleton.*"

"You've had a heck of a week, running up on Sister Clare's body like that, and then the *other...*"

"Yes, siree, it's been kinda'..." Frank Sr. trailed off.

"I'm sorry you had to witness all that. Once you've seen something like that, well, it's hard to get it out of your head." He dropped in an onion and a cucumber and handed the sack to Frank Sr.

"I don't mind telling you, I didn't sleep a wink that first night," Frank Sr. volunteered.

"How about you, Frank Jr.?" Olivera said.

He stared back fixedly, as if surprised or offended by the question. "Oh, well, I been sleepin' all right."

Frank Sr. looked around at his son. "You told me you hadn't slept good all week."

Frank Jr. glanced away, didn't respond at first to his father's contradiction, but then blurted out, "It ain't every day you see a dead nun lying in your path."

"Well, men, I didn't mean to hold you up." Olivera reached in his pocket for his billfold. "I'm sure you've got plenty to do, it being the beginning of the harvest and all."

"Yeah, as a matter of fact we do." Frank Jr. picked up the last box of vegetables and set it on the truck bed. "Daddy, I'm ready when you are." He tipped his hat to Olivera and climbed in the cab.

"Just a second, Lieutenant." Frank Sr. placed a hand on Olivera's arm and lowered his voice. "What about the bones them fellers toted off? They gonna' be able to figure out who it was?"

"You'd be surprised what they can work out these days, from a skeleton or a bone or even a chip of a bone."

"If that don't beat all." He slapped his hat against his leg.

"We don't know *who* it is, not yet. But, between Dr. McGinnis and the professors, we've got a good idea who it *might* be. I don't mean we've got a name, but we know a good bit about him."

"You don't say." Frank Sr. shook his head.

"Come to think of it, Frank, you might be able to help us with the identification, well, narrow down the possibilities. You worked for the Bilyeus back in the sixties and seventies, didn't you? I recall your saying something about knowing Ninon since she was a child."

"Yes, sir. I've known the Bilyeus going way, way back. Mr. Jake, Mr. Arnold. My family sharecropped on Mr. Jake's place when Ninon was born."

"So maybe you knew the John Doe skeleton."

"John Doe skeleton?" he repeated.

"The coroner says he's African American." Olivera handed Frank Sr. a ten-dollar bill.

He tucked it in his bib pocket. "There was that one feller went missin'."

He waited in silence, hoping to hear something pertinent to the subject at hand.

"Eugene Brown was his name." Frank Sr. scratched his head. "There're a bunch of Browns still around here, if you wanted to ask 'em about it."

Olivera reached for his tablet. "You knew this man, Eugene Brown?"

"Sure, I knowed him. He worked for Mr. Jake. He was older than me. He run off to Memphis—least that's what people said. Never came back."

"And was never heard from again?"

"Not as far as I heard."

"You wouldn't happen to know the names of any of his people?"

"One of his nieces was out there the other day when, uh, me and Frank Jr. were working on the cistern. The woman who works for Mr. John Earle."

"Ms. Frye's friend?"

"That's the one. Smiley...Saffron Smiley."

"Don't suppose you've seen her around here today, have you?" He glanced back at the empty square.

"Naw, but I saw Mosey. She was here just a minute ago."

"She mention where she was headed?"

"Let me ask Frank Jr. if he remembers. Frank," he called, "where'd Mosey say she was goin'?"

"To the lake, Daddy. Said she and her husband were headed to the lake."

"Yep," Frank Sr. confirmed. "I picked her out a watermelon, and I think she did mention something about being on her way to the lake. You can probably catch 'em if you hurry."

Olivera thanked him for the information and walked away from the stall, bag in one hand, cell phone in the other. He stopped and set the vegetables on a bench, then called Mosey.

"Lieutenant Olivera here," he said. "Sorry to bother you on a Friday afternoon."

"No bother, Lieutenant. What can I do for you?"

"I need Ms. Smiley's phone number, if you happen to have it."

"I'll text it to you."

"Okay, good. Thanks."

"I thought you might be calling for something else." Here it goes. "What's that?"

"I've got some information for you—didn't Robert tell you?"

"Yes, he mentioned something about Mr. Lobos."

"He's in town. Did you know that?"

"Yes, I spoke to him this morning, so see—"

"Did he tell you," she interrupted, "why he came to Hembree?"

"Yes, he filled me in on all that, but I'll be at the station Monday morning, should you feel the need—"

"Okay, Lieutenant. Monday morning, I'll drop by around 10:00."

"You might call first."

"Sure thing. Bye then."

As he spoke, he had moved toward a row of crape myrtles in the middle of the square and taken a seat on a stone bench, shaded and cool to the touch. He set his purchases to one side and watched the older Ferguson as he finished loading the truck. Frank Sr. had either done a fine job of acting or knew nothing about the John Doe murder. But he wasn't quite ready to cross his name off the list, not just yet. He pulled out his map, unchanged since he'd sketched in the trunk and the hole in the ground. He studied the card from side to side, then up and down. He held it at arm's length. Then he placed it on the bench and traced the path that led from the bare patch of ground to the hermitage, then branched off to the right and entered the woods. With his index finger, he scanned every row of the dead nun's garden. "That's odd," he muttered, looking up. "That's *very* odd."

"What's odd, Lieutenant?"

"Ms. Frye, I thought you and Robert were on your way to the lake."

"The watermelon wasn't ripe. I would've thought Frank Sr. capable of picking out a perfect watermelon, wouldn't you? But, as luck would have it, he was off his game. So—"

"—you came back for another one. I hate to tell you, but, as you can see, the vendors have closed up for the day." He pointed toward the row of empty parking spaces.

She ignored his remark and, instead, peeked into the bag that sat beside him.

"Nice tomatoes, Lieutenant."

"I thought so."

An awkward pause followed during which he realized he'd either have to stand or offer Ms. Frye a seat. "Won't you sit down?"

"Don't mind if I do. I have to wait for Robert. He's coming back to pick me up." As she sat, she glanced across at the card he was holding. "Hey, an index card. I haven't seen one of those in ages. I do everything on the computer nowadays, but in high school my English teacher made us take notes for our term papers on index cards."

"Well, I don't use them much, but every now and again I find them useful."

"I see you do. What's that, if you don't mind my asking?"

"Oh, nothing. Just a map. Well, I call it a map but actually it's a picture—I guess you could call it a picture."

"Of the hermitage, looks like. Just like it. That's a good sketch, Lieutenant."

"You think so?"

"Yeah, I do." She cocked her head. "That's the cottage, and there's Sister Clare's little garden and the path leading to the church. May I see it a second?"

"No harm, I guess. I was trying to sketch the crime scene, as a way of, uh—"

"As a way of fixing it in your mind? I've done that."

"You have?"

"Sure, doesn't everybody?"

"I wouldn't know." He held out his hand, waiting for her to return the card.

"Look at that." She moved the card away. "An old

trunk."

He dropped his hand to his knee.

"I'm a fiend for old trunks." Her eyes widened.

"You are?" he said, as if he didn't know.

"Don't you remember? I found that picture in an old trunk at the antique shop. The panorama torn in two—that one of the Hansbrough estate. Nadia has a ton of old trunks—"

Surprise, surprise….

"—but she's not like me." Her eyes slid from the card to Olivera, who had begun to squirm. "She buys them to sell. You ought to see that back room of hers. She's got 'em stacked all the way to the ceiling. I much prefer the stuff inside—old photographs, old linens. I don't suppose—"

"What?"

"—you found anything of interest in *that* trunk. It must have been Sister Clare's, right? I wouldn't think a nun would have much in the way of possessions."

"Yes, it was hers. Well, I'm assuming it was hers."

"Because it was in *her* garden."

"If you put it that way."

"Doesn't make much sense really, does it? We're always assuming, but there's no obvious reason to assume, unless—"

"Unless what?"

"She said it was hers, or her initials were on it, or only she knew it was there," she rattled off. "Was it buried?"

"Yes, it was buried, right there in that back corner of the garden. The hole's right there, see?" He pointed to the hole.

"Who dug it up—do you know?" She handed him

back the card.

"That's not entirely clear. I'm assuming she did."

"That's funny."

"What's funny?"

"If she dug it up, where's the shovel?"

He stared at Mosey, and she stared back at him, blue eyes defiantly meeting brown.

"Ms. Frye, I'd have to say you've read my mind. I was thinking exactly that, just now, before you came up." He hadn't meant to say it like that—or maybe he had—but that's how it came out.

She took the hint and stood. "Oh, I suppose I've interrupted you."

He stood, too. "Not at all, I—"

"That's okay. I ought to be watching for Robert."

"But before you go," he said, "if you don't mind, I'd like to ask you, uh, something of a somewhat delicate nature. It concerns the investigation, but since you're already privy to certain things…"

"What was it you wanted to know?"

"Ms. Smiley—"

"Saffron."

"Yes, Saffron Smiley. I have reason to believe—"

"Oh, no." Mosey covered her mouth.

"Yes, I'm afraid we may have some bad news."

"Her great-great-uncle…" She collapsed onto the bench. "She told me the other day she had a feeling it was her great-great uncle."

"That's what I suspect. His name was Eugene Brown. He worked at Larkspur a good many years ago."

"Eugene Brown. She was afraid it was he. He went off somewhere, Memphis, they thought, and was never heard from again." She looked up at Olivera, who was still standing. "You should talk to Saffron. I texted you her number. She spoke to Eugene's brother just this week."

"His brother?"

"Patrick Brown, but, before you contact Mr. Brown, please speak to Saffron. His health is failing, and the shock, well…"

"Yes, of course. I'll speak to her first."

At the blast of a car horn, both looked around.

"That's Robert," Mosey said. "I'd better run. You call Saffron. She'll tell you what you need to know."

"Thanks. I'll be in touch," he said as Mosey went rushing off. He sat back down on the bench. "Why'd I say that?" he mumbled. Just one of those things people say automatically, he mused, like when a waiter says "enjoy your dinner" and the customer replies "you, too." Nonsensical, that *I'll be in touch*, because the last thing he wanted to do was get in touch with Mosey Frye, if he could avoid it. It was his great hope to solve the murders of Ninon Bilyeu and John Doe without any help from anyone, but what a joke that was. Yes, what a joke. Carlotta Humphrey, Eads McGinnis, Nadia Abboud. All, in their own way, had helped move the case along. "Downright irritating," he said, but it was a concession he had to make. "What a snoop, what an interfering busy-body," he mumbled, grabbing his sack of vegetables and heading off to his car. "Where's the shovel?" he drawled. "Where's the *dang* shovel?"

Chapter Twenty-Four

Friday, September 25, late afternoon
Olivera's house

Olivera grabbed a sieve from under the sink and dumped in the contents of his sack—a half dozen ripe tomatoes, a cucumber, a bell pepper, and an onion. He opened the faucet and flooded the vegetables with cold water.

"Mil-ly, kitty-kitty-kitty."

He propped his radio on the windowsill behind the sink and tuned in the Razorback game just as the fans were calling the Hogs. "Wooooooo, Pig!" He raised his arms high and wiggled his fingers. "Wooooooo, Pig! Sooie! Razorbacks!"

Grim Milly Grimalkin, who was napping on a chair cushion under the table, lifted her head and gave him a withering look.

"Want some gazpacho?" He picked her up and rubbed her wooly head against his cheek. "No, I don't suppose you do. I know what *you* want." He opened the refrigerator, grabbed an open can of Chic Cuisine, and passed it under her pink nose.

Most cats would have purred, but not Milly. As usual, she uttered one loud "waaanh," similar to the high-pitched cry of a baby doll.

He filled her bowl with food, and she ate it up

quickly. Apparently wanting something else, she fixed her gaze on Olivera. But before he could respond, she leapt to the sink and drank from the dripping faucet.

"Get down from there." He set her next to her water dish. "You wait."

"Waaanh!"

"Waaanh, yourself, you silly cat." He filled the dish, then washed his hands and placed the vegetables on the cutting board. "Now," he laid down his knife, "I'm going to tell you what I found out today. Not everything, but I will tell you this. DeGroat did not kill your momma, neither did his Uncle Antoine. A. B. is a snooty old man, but he's not a killer. You should have seen his nephew—ha!—dressed to the nines for an evening at the Tavernette—ha! A distant cousin, Rafael de Lobos—" He paused, squatting next to Milly. "Do you know what that means? Raphael of the Wolves. And you know what wolves do to cats?"

"Waaanh."

"That's right." Olivera uttered a low growl. "But this wolf was harmless. He wouldn't kill a fly, much less an adorable cat. Yes, you are," he crooned.

He returned to his chopping, and once he'd filled the food processor to within a couple of inches of the brim, he flipped on the power switch, which sent Milly scrambling for cover behind the sideboard.

"All in all," he raised his voice over the roar of the processor, "I have managed to eliminate three suspects today." He turned off the machine and poured the purée into a ricer. "Yum, yum, yum." He set the ricer over a bowl and slowly cranked the handle till the consistency was silky smooth. "I know you don't care for gazpacho, but you're missing out on something delicious." He added oil and vinegar and a couple of grinds of pepper and salt. He stirred and took a taste. "*Qué sabroso*." He covered the bowl with a tea towel and placed it in the refrigerator. "Hey, Milly, join me for a drink while the gazpacho cools?"

She remained behind the sideboard.

"No? Don't care for the hard stuff?" He filled a tall glass with ice cubes, poured in a couple of fingers of vodka, and topped it off with a splash of dry gin. "As I was saying, I have crossed several names off my list. The distant cousins—the lot of them—and Mannix, which leaves Father Moody and the Fergusons. So, who do you think did it, huh?"

She held her tongue.

"No opinion? But, if anyone knows, you do." He picked up the radio and his drink and headed for the porch. "You coming?"

She emerged from her bunker and, dashing in front of him, led the way through the dining room and foyer and out the side door to the porch. But before he could situate himself on the wicker lounge chair, she slipped in ahead of him and curled against the throw pillows.

"Not your chair, Milly. Down!" He scooped her up and plopped her on the floor, then sat. "Okay, come on." He patted his lap.

Superfluous his invitation, for before he could get the words out of his mouth, she alighted on the chair arm, looked him in the eye, and held it for a good half-minute. She wanted to talk, he assumed, but, having no idea how to manage it, resorted to prolonged stares.

"So, who was it?" He brought the reciprocal gaze to an end. "One of the Fergusons or Father Moody? If you aren't sure, give me your best guess."

She continued staring but without a sound.

Olivera sipped his drink and listened to the game, shouting, cursing occasionally, and banging pillows against the porch wall. "Milly, they're throwing the game away! Do you understand?"

"Waaanh." She leapt from the lounge chair to the rocker, curled up, and closed her eyes.

"Time for gazpacho." He got up from the chaise, but before he could reach the refrigerator, a knock came at the front door, to which he turned instead. He peeped through the drapes. It was Carlotta Humphrey. "A tad unexpected," he mumbled on his way to the door. "Ms. Humphrey."

"Oh, please, Lieutenant," she said in a slow drawl, "call me Carlotta."

"As you wish. Come in, won't you?" He stepped away from the door into the cavernous parlor, which was empty of furnishings except for a floor lamp. When he switched it on, a whirlpool of pale circles spread over the dark-stained wood.

"Nice floors," she said. She set a bottle of wine on the mantel above the white brick fireplace and looked around. "How long you been living here?"

He smiled. "I suppose you noticed the absence of furniture." He chuckled. "I don't entertain much. And in fact, you're my first guest. I was about to have a bowl of gazpacho." He picked up the bottle of wine and, with a sweep of his hand, indicated the path to the kitchen. "Will you join me?"

"Well, just for a minute. I don't want to interrupt your supper."

"Wouldn't you like to try my gazpacho? I bought the vegetables today at the farmers market."

He placed the wine on the table, then set out the gazpacho, bowls, spoons, wine glasses, and French bread. "Perfect accompaniment for gazpacho." He filled the glasses and, raising his, said, "To my first guest."

She clinked his glass. "So, why am I here?—you must be wondering."

"Care for some bread?"

She pulled a piece off the crusty loaf. "Thank you."

"I suppose you would need a reason to come knocking on a single man's door on a Friday night."

"Yes, actually, I would." She smiled.

"So?"

"I happened to see Frank Ferguson. He mentioned you were at the Square earlier today, knocking on *my* door."

"True." He took a taste of the cool purée.

"Well?"

"I confess," he said. "I wanted to ask a favor— related to the Bilyeu case, of course."

"And what was that?"

He paused. Human remains didn't make for good dinner conversation, but he plowed ahead, sensing Carlotta wasn't squeamish. "It's about the John Doe skeleton they pulled out of the cistern at Larkspur."

She nodded and sipped her gazpacho.

"We have a good bit to go on. Time of death, sex, race, maybe even the deceased's initial." He broke off a piece of bread and dipped it in the soup. "Oh, and a guitar pick and a belt buckle engraved with a treble clef. Looks like our victim is a middle-aged African American male, maybe a musician, somebody around here in the late sixties or early seventies."

"And you're assuming, given the remains were

found at Larkspur—"

"—that he was known around the plantation."

"I don't have all the records," she said, "but I think I do have the ones going back as far as Mr. Jake's time. My stepfather and step-brother worked pretty closely with the Bilyeus. But by the time I came on the scene, Jake and Arnold had passed. I'd be glad to take a look, see if I can come up with something. What was the initial?"

"As best we could tell, looked like a B, D, or R. The watch case was pretty scratched up."

"Hmm." She took a sip of wine. "I know the Browns sharecropped on the place for a good many years."

"That's what I hear, and chances are Eugene Brown is, in fact, our John Doe."

"He worked for Mr. Arnold?"

"Possibly, but McGinnis says the joints, especially the knees and ankles, suggest John Doe was *not* a farm worker. Frank Ferguson knew Brown and said he went missing, never came back to Hembree, as far as he knew."

"Have you spoken to the family?"

"Not yet. Well, I've spoken to one relative but not about this. I'll do that first thing tomorrow."

"So, what do you want me to do?" she said.

"Check out the records for that time period—late sixties, early seventies—and get me a list of anyone who worked or lived at Larkspur, anyone associated with the Bilyeus."

"But you're pretty sure the deceased is Eugene Brown."

Olivera didn't answer.

Carlotta raised an eyebrow. "I get it. You think the

killer's name is there, too."

"Yes, that's exactly what I'm thinking."

Chapter Twenty-Five

Monday, September 28
Hembree Police Station

On Sunday, Olivera alerted Springer to the urgency of his plan. He and Reagan were to meet him at the police station early Monday morning, ready to launch a search of the hermitage and surrounding property.

The officers arrived at the station around seven to start the preliminaries, and when Olivera came in, Springer announced proudly, "We've rounded up three dogs, Chief. We got Bud and Martha, and Mound City is sending over Dan—ha, they call him Lieutenant Dan. Sergeant Farr'll be here any minute."

"Listen up," Olivera said. He deposited his briefcase on the reception desk. "I want you men to start tracking at the hermitage. Be sure to take a sample of Ninon's blood with you—don't forget."

"Her blood?"

"Put your eyes back in their sockets, Springer. Yes, her blood. If we were looking for tracks or a body, it'd be different, but we're looking for blood, *her* blood. The assailant was likely to have blood on him somewhere— his shoes, his hands at the very least. It's unlikely he had time to give the shovel a thorough cleaning, so we'll probably pick up some prints on the handle. If you find it, package it, and get it back to the lab pronto—you understand?"

Both men nodded.

"And if you *do* find it," he added, "look around for whatever else the perp might have dropped. Cigarette butts, matches, a gum wrapper, anything—and package that, too."

"If you don't mind my asking," Springer said, "why are we looking for a shovel?"

"Somebody re-buried the trunk, right? So, what'd he do with the shovel?"

"O-o-h, I see what you mean, Chief. When me and Reagan were digging up the garden, we used our own shovels. Wonder what happened to Sister Clare's."

"It didn't walk off by itself," Reagan volunteered, with a waggle of his head.

Springer had struck a pensive look, but, at his partner's comment, it contorted into a smirk. "It didn't walk off by itself," he mocked, "didn't walk off by itself."

Olivera shot an exasperated look at the two of them, then went on to remind them of Moody's statement that he'd seen Sister Clare digging in her garden the morning of the murder.

"That's right," Springer said. "And she had to have a shovel to dig up the trunk in the first place."

"She sure did," Reagan agreed.

"And the perp probably would've used a shovel to bury it," Olivera said.

"But why'd he take the shovel with him?" Reagan said.

"Think about it." Springer looked at Reagan. "If you'd knocked somebody off and buried the murder weapon...Well, someone must have come up while he was there. He had the shovel in his hand and just ran with it. Makes sense to me."

"Yeah, I suppose it does," Reagan agreed.

"But then," Springer continued, "to avoid getting caught with the shovel, he just pitched it somewhere, tall grass, a ditch…"

"That's the theory," Olivera confirmed. "Keeping that in mind, you need to think about the perp's get-away route. Which way he was likely to run."

"That depends," Springer said. "Suppose he came in a car."

"Yeah, or a truck." Reagan said.

"He probably, uh, tossed it somewhere along the road," Springer suggested.

"True," Olivera said. "If you don't find anything on the grounds, follow the road from the church toward the outskirts of town. You're not likely to find it in plain sight. Look for patches of brush, trees…"

"There aren't a lot trees." Springer shook his head. "Nothing but cotton fields all along there."

"Which is to our advantage," Olivera said. "And when Farr gets here with that dog of his, you guys head out and report back to me as soon as you find anything, anything at all. You got that?"

"Certainly, Chief. Don't you worry. If there's a shovel out there, we'll find it."

"The shovel's our priority, but don't stop there. Have a look around."

"Sure thing, Chief."

Olivera grabbed his briefcase and walked back to his office, picking up a coffee on the way. He needed to call Saffron Smiley. Might as well get it over with. He dialed Shepherd Realty, and Saffron answered. "Ms. Smiley, this is Lieutenant Olivera. I need to speak to you as soon as possible. Could you come to the station?"

"What's this about, Lieutenant?"

"I'd rather not discuss it on the phone."

"Okay, I'll be there, soon as I can get someone to cover the front desk."

Within the half hour, she appeared at his door.

"Come on in, Ms. Smiley. I appreciate your coming over."

"No problem, Lieutenant. I got Mosey to cover for me."

Hearing a tinge of apprehension in her voice, he lowered his eyes. "Well…what I have to say is not good. Maybe you already suspect that."

Saffron stared at him straight-faced, as if she knew nothing, not even where she was. Or if she did know something, she wasn't saying, not to him anyway.

"Take a seat, please." He pointed to the folding chair by his desk. "The remains we found at the Bilyeu place, well, there was evidence located near the remains. We found a belt buckle, a guitar pick, and a watch." He unzipped a plastic envelope and emptied the contents. "The watch is engraved with an initial." He passed her the piece. "Can you tell me anything about it?"

She picked up the watch and opened and closed it. She turned it over. Her expression wilted. "I suppose you think that's a B."

Olivera nodded.

"I guess it could be." She laid the watch down and looked at the pick. "I can tell you that my great-great-uncle—who I never knew, mind you—played the guitar. But I'm not sure that means anything."

Next, she looked at the buckle and confirmed what

McGinnis had suggested. "That looks like a treble clef."
She nodded slowly. "All this stuff could have belonged
to Eugene Brown—could have—but who am I to say?
Show it to somebody who knew him, like his brother, T.
Patrick Brown."

"I heard he's in a nursing home."

"He's out at Magnolia, but he's pretty sharp. He told
me most of what I know about Uncle Eugene."

"I hear Eugene Brown worked for the Bilyeus.
Maybe you could fill me in on that."

"He worked for Mr. Jake before the war. My whole
family did."

"World War II?" Olivera said.

"That's right."

"Did he only work for Jake, not Arnold?"

"I don't think he worked for Mr. Arnold. He left
Hembree after the war."

"Did anybody know why he left?"

"Uncle T. Patrick said he didn't get along with Mr.
Jake."

"Why was that?"

"He joined the sharecroppers union."

"He must have known the organizer José de Lobos,"
he interjected.

"He did. They were pretty good friends."

"Hmm. And you say Mr. Brown left and never came
back?"

She nodded.

"And nobody knew *why* he left?"

"He didn't like farming. He said he was going to
Memphis, get a job at a club, play the guitar."

"The coroner is checking the local medical records.
We're hoping to confirm the deceased's identity that

way. But we might have to resort to DNA. If that be the case, we would want to get a sample from his brother."

She heaved a sigh. "Would it be possible for me to get that for you, Lieutenant?"

He paused to think. A little irregular, yes, but if he could avoid upsetting the victim's elderly brother... "I suppose that'd be all right, given the circumstances. You could bring us a saliva sample on a glass. Slip it into a plastic bag, avoiding contamination, of course. Might be the easiest way. He wouldn't have to know."

"You don't need his permission?"

"For evidence taken from a glass, no. But maybe we won't have to resort to that, if the medical records pan out."

She took a handkerchief from her tote and wiped her eyes.

"I know this is upsetting," Olivera said.

"Uncle T. is so old." She shook her head. "To have to find out now..."

"Well, when a loved one is missing, sometimes it's better to know."

"I suppose, but if it turns out he was murdered..." Her face fell.

He returned the items to the envelope. "Ms. Smiley, I am truly sorry to prolong this, but if you could answer a few more questions."

"Certainly. I'll tell you what I can."

"Do you know if Eugene Brown had any enemies? Did he get along with his family, the workers on the place?"

"Uncle Eugene got mixed up in the sharecroppers strike, and after that, he and Mr. Jake—"

"Was he arrested for that?" he cut in.

"I don't think so. All Uncle T. said was that Eugene and Mr. Jake didn't see eye to eye. But he thought Eugene would have left regardless. He didn't want to farm. He wanted to be a musician and figured Memphis was the place to go."

It puzzled Olivera that nothing had come of his disappearance, but he kept that to himself. He assured Saffron he'd be in touch as soon as he knew anything. "And if we get a positive identification," he added, "I may need to ask you a few more questions."

In the course of Saffron's explanation, he'd realized how little he knew of the region's history. He had a general idea of the labor movement of the twenties and thirties but understood little about how it had affected sharecroppers in the Delta.

Saffron rose to leave. "Lieutenant, before I go, may I ask you something?"

"Of course."

"If this *is* my great-great-uncle, the family will want to give him a Christian burial."

Olivera pushed back from his desk and stood. "As soon as we make the identification, the coroner will release the remains."

"Do you know how he died?"

"We can't be sure, but the evidence suggests he might have been stabbed."

"Stabbed." She wiped her eyes again. "I don't guess we'll ever know who did it."

"We're still gathering evidence, but we may know something soon."

"You mean there's a possibility—?"

"A possibility, yes, but I'd rather not say any more on that point just yet. Should we get sufficient evidence, anything substantial, I'll be in touch."

"Thank you, Lieutenant. And please let me know about the burial."

He handed her his card. "I will."

Chapter Twenty-Six

Monday, September 28, morning
Frye, Frye, and Humphrey

Olivera, having completed his Monday morning tasks, sat idly at his desk waiting for Springer's call. He needed to speak to Carlotta, but instead of calling, thought he'd walk over to Frye, Frye, and Humphrey.

Dot met him at the door. "Come in, Lieutenant. Carlotta said you might drop by. How's the investigation going?"

He smiled and handed her his hat. "Things seem to be coming to a head pretty quickly."

"Well, I'm glad to hear that. Can I get you some coffee while you wait?"

"If you've got some made."

"I've just brewed a pot."

He glanced over at the closed door to Carlotta's office. "Is Ms. Humphrey with a client?"

"She's on the phone. I don't think it'll be long. Have a seat."

He sat in the same spot where he'd sat several days earlier. He leaned back, stretched out his legs, and pondered what the rest of the day might bring. Was he being overly optimistic to believe, as he'd just told Dot, that everything was coming to a head? Would he know by the end of the day who killed Ninon Bilyeu and, with that revelation, maybe who killed Eugene Brown? Even if the evidence they'd gathered was circumstantial, that skeleton *was* Brown—had to be. He crossed himself and sent up a prayer for dental records, his best prospect for a quick identification.

Dot brought his coffee, along with packets of cream and sugar, and set it on the table in front of the sofa. "Can I get you anything else, Lieutenant?"

"Thank you. This is fine." He reached for a packet of sugar. No sooner had he broken it open, Carlotta pushed back the door to the inner office and invited him in.

"I managed to get through the whole stack of files," she said with a sigh, "and I've found something you're gonna want to see." She had a look of fatigued contentment, as if she'd just finished an exam and was confident she'd passed. "Come on in." She shuffled a couple of sheets into a folder and seated herself across from Olivera. "I started in the sixties, which is when the incident occurred, correct?"

"That's what Ellison and Jessup tell us." He stirred his coffee.

"And I went to the end of the seventies."

He nodded.

"I have more records, but I didn't see the point."

"Right, no point in going past the seventies. Tell me, what did you look at exactly?"

"Wills, titles, financial records. I've pinned down who worked and when. No problem with that. Who was paid what, who was loaned money, and so on. It's all straightforward—the Bilyeus were good record keepers. Nothing sloppy about any of it. The Fergusons and the Browns sharecropped—we already knew that—and I didn't see anything irregular concerning their work, pay, or accommodations. No unpaid debts, nothing that might have caused a ruckus." She pulled a sheet off the top of the stack. "The one thing I *did* find that seemed a little irregular—at least, to me it did—was an unexpected name." She passed the sheet to Olivera. "Next to the yellow tab—you see it?"

"Uh-*huh*." He looked at Carlotta. "Melvin Moody."

She nodded.

His brow lifted. "So, in what capacity...?"

"There's nothing very specific." She reached for the document. "It says 'workman,' nothing more. He was in Mr. Arnold's employ from June, 1969 to March, 1970."

"Uh-huh."

She stared over her readers at Olivera.

"What'd he do, I wonder?"

"Well, it doesn't really say, but, whatever it was, he was paid handsomely for it." She waggled her brows.

Olivera leaned forward. "This figure here?"

"That figure. A nice sum for the seventies, wouldn't you say?"

"Two thousand dollars. Yes, sir, a good bit for then." He took out his note pad and jotted down the sum. "So that's it?" As soon as he'd said it, he knew it was a peculiar thing to say, considering the importance of her findings. "Well, I mean, anything else, besides this possibly *vital* bit of information?"

"That's it," she said.

He took a sip of coffee and, standing, thanked her for her help.

"Are we getting close to knowing what's what?" She leaned in and began gathering files.

"I wish I knew."

"No positive identification on the skeleton?"

"Not yet. I need to speak to Dr. McGinnis to see how that's coming. I talked to Saffron Smiley this morning, and she couldn't give a positive ID on the objects found in the cistern."

"Sounds to me, Lieutenant, like you're an inch away from solving the case...two cases."

"One thing puzzles me." He took a step toward the door. "If the skeleton turns out to be Eugene Brown, what was he doing back in Hembree? According to Ms. Smiley, he left after the war and never came back."

"Well, I can't help you with that. I didn't run across any mention of Eugene Brown in the records. Maybe he popped in and popped out without anybody knowing."

"Or popped in and got himself stabbed."

Carlotta edged closer and lowered her voice. "Surely not, Lieutenant," she said. "Surely not," as if denial would make the possibility disappear.

"I'll know soon enough." He picked up his cup and followed her into the outer office. "Thanks, Dot," he said as he placed the cup on the end table.

"Nice to see you, Lieutenant," Dot said.

On his way out, he turned to say goodbye to Carlotta, but she had gone back into her office and half-closed the door.

Reaching the street, he checked his watch. It was a little soon to call Springer, who'd been gone less than an hour. But he might give McGinnis a call. He pulled out his phone. "Dr. McGinnis," he said. "Olivera here."

"I suppose you're calling about the records."

"I am. Find anything?"

"We got a match on Brown's dental records."

"Excellent. I spoke to Ms. Smiley this morning. She

was willing to get DNA evidence for us, but now—"

"—we can spare her that ordeal."

"We certainly can. And listen, go ahead and release the remains…Ninon's body as well. I don't see any reason—"

"—nor do I."

"We've got everything we need. I'll contact the Browns, and if you'd let Bilyeu and DeGroat know, or if you prefer, just give Ms. Humphrey a call. She can get a message to them."

He slipped his phone into his pocket, then pulled it out again to call the department. "Ms. Hill, any news from Springer?"

"Nothing yet, Lieutenant."

"If he calls, tell him I'm on my way out there. Tell him there's been a development in the case, and I need to speak to, well, one of the witnesses right away."

"Anything else?"

"Nothing else. I'll fill him in when I get there."

A short while later, Olivera arrived at St. Mary's and parked in front of the church. Father Moody was at the door, as if anticipating his arrival. "Father Moody, I'm glad I caught you," he said, as he crossed the gravel lot.

"You can catch me here just about any moment of the day." His face was placid, as if he hadn't a care in the world.

"Not a bad place to be, right?"

"Not a bad place at all." He rocked back and forth on his heels. "What brings you here?"

"I've got a few more questions, if you don't mind."

"Certainly. Shall we step inside? It's cooler and more comfortable."

He followed Moody into the foyer and, then, into a

223

cell-like room on the left. It was cooler, yes. But more comfortable? Undoubtedly, it was not. Like Mannix's inner sanctum, it was sparsely furnished with a wooden platform for a desk, three wooden benches, and a file cabinet.

"Take a seat." Moody pointed to a bench below a small window, then drew water from a water cooler for Olivera and himself. "Have some water, Lieutenant. It's hot today. One must stay hydrated."

"Thank you, Father." He accepted the glass and sat.

Moody sat at the make-shift desk. "You've made progress?"

"Yes and no."

"I see. I suppose it's difficult, I mean, having so little to go on."

"We have more evidence than you might imagine but not the *right* evidence."

"The right evidence?" The priest's peridot eyes looked tired.

"The victims' identities, when they were killed, how they were killed—we know all that. But not *who* killed them or *why*." He watched for a reaction.

"In a murder investigation, that must be everything."

"Opportunity, that, too, is key. In Sister Clare's case, a number of people had opportunity. You, for example, had opportunity. But in the case of Eugene Brown—"

"Eugene Brown. He was the other victim?" he said casually.

"Yes, did you know Mr. Brown?"

"I knew—know—some of the Browns, but Eugene, I don't believe I knew him."

"Never had occasion to see him at Larkspur?"

"Larkspur?"

"I believe you worked there once. Am I wrong?"

"No, Lieutenant, you are not wrong. I worked there briefly a long, long time ago, soon after I left home."

"I understand that you were paid handsomely for your work. Exactly what did you do for Mr. Bilyeu, if you don't mind my asking?"

His body stiffened. "I'd rather not say, Lieutenant. My association with Mr. Bilyeu was of a private nature."

"Of course, as a priest you must have a great many things you must hold in confidence."

"Yes, of course. That's the nature of our work." His tone altered slightly from neutral to self-justifying.

"But you weren't a priest then."

"As I said, I was just out of school." Moody drank his water to the bottom of the glass. "You care for more water, Lieutenant?"

"No, thanks." Olivera rose and placed his glass on the bench next to Moody's. "You know, Father, back at the station, I have a small pyx that was given to me when I left Santa Clara. It's a souvenir from the mission. When St. Clare's convent was under threat from enemy soldiers—you must know the story, Father—she placed the consecrated host in a pyx and then placed the pyx on the convent wall. The soldiers spotted it and became frightened, uh, knowing its contents. They fled, leaving the Holy Mother and her nuns undisturbed. Do you know the story? I'm sure you must."

"Yes, I'm familiar with the history of the Poor Clares. You're aware that Sister Clare was a member of the order."

"So I've been told. It's unfortunate she was alone, unprotected."

Moody looked up at Olivera. "Very sad." His eyes

narrowed.

"Too bad there wasn't some *thing*, like a pyx, to frighten enemies away. She never mentioned to you that she was afraid?" Olivera, who was still standing, turned away from the priest and toward the mournful sound of baying dogs. "Did you hear that, Father?"

"Hunters, I imagine."

Moody stood and looked out the window, which was high above the bench where Olivera had been sitting.

"Where were we?" Olivera cleared his throat.

Moody sat back down. "I think, Lieutenant, we've already talked about this, at the police station. I recall you asked me—"

"Yes, I suppose we did," Olivera said.

"Was there anything else?"

"No, not really. Just that one point, about your work at Larkspur. But let me be honest. I'm a little surprised you didn't mention that—that you'd once worked for Ninon's father."

"I guess it slipped my mind. It isn't important to the case, is it?"

"Important to the case?" His eyes flicked from one side of the cell to the other, as if the answer were displayed there somewhere. "Hard to say, Father, hard to say. Could be important. Sometimes a negligible bit of information…" He left the insinuation floating there in the dank air and, picking up his hat, fanned himself. "I suppose that's all for now. I need to get going." He took a step toward the door, then turned and faced the priest. "You may be hearing from the families. The Bilyeus and the Browns are anxious to give their loved ones a Christian burial. I'm sure they'll be in touch—both families are Catholic. There must be a lot of Bilyeus and

Browns on the rolls of St. Mary of the Angels."

Moody's facial expression twisted for a second. He remained behind the desk. "Bilyeus and Browns? Well, at one time there must have been."

"No more Bilyeus in Hembree, except Sister Clare's cousins, for the moment."

"They're here now?"

"Oh, yes, and anxious to see her assailant brought to justice." He approached the door, and Moody stood.

"Don't bother, Father. I can see myself out."

"No bother, Lieutenant. Please come again."

Olivera headed for the squad car. With only trees between him and the dogs, the baying was louder. He opened the car door and looked back to see Moody silhouetted in the doorway. He didn't applaud. He wouldn't, of course. But he was sorely tempted, given the performance he'd just witnessed. The man's feigned detachment, as if none of it had anything to do with him, was all too obvious.

He drove away in the direction of the hounds, turned right onto the main road, and edged toward the clearing in front of the hermitage. He downshifted to first and lowered the windows. The dogs, he speculated, were a good hundred yards away. He shifted into second and drove along slowly until he caught sight of the officers a short distance from the road. "Springer!" he yelled.

"Over here, Chief!"

He got out and eased his way down an embankment at the side of the road.

"We got it, Lieutenant. Martha found it, right over there," Springer pointed, "behind that clump of trees."

Reagan lifted the shovel with gloved hands.

"Good job, men. Did you find anything else?"

"Not yet," Springer said.

Olivera nodded to the taller of the three officers. "Thank you, Farr, for driving over and, uh, bringing Lieutenant Dan."

"Any time, Lieutenant. Me and Dan spend as much time afield as we can. Not much going on back in Mound City. They tell me you got two homicides over here."

"Yes, and looks like we're about to solve at least one of them."

"The perp is from around here?" Farr said.

"Possibly, and if we can lift some prints off this shovel…"

"It could've been lying out in the open for 'bout a week," Springer said. "Reckon we'll get anything?"

"I bet we can. I'll take it back to the lab and see what we've got. Springer, you and Reagan stay here and keep looking. Lieutenant Farr, if you need to be getting back…"

"I'm here. Might as well stay till we finish."

"I'd appreciate that. If we can't get prints off the shovel, any other physical evidence could be critical."

"No problem, Lieutenant," Farr said.

"We'll give this whole area a good going over," Reagan said, arms spread wide.

Olivera, shovel in hand, climbed the embankment and sped away toward Hembree.

Chapter Twenty-Seven

Monday, September 28, noon
Hembree Police Station

The traces of blood on the shovel matched Ninon
Bilyeu's blood type, and the sets of fingerprints matched
those of the victim and Melvin Moody. Moody wouldn't
be able to claim he'd only borrowed the shovel, given his
prints were in the victim's blood.

"We've got him dead to rights, Springer, but I need
to pick up a warrant. I'll get over to Judge Hendricks's
office, and you and Reagan go back to St. Mary's and
keep an eye on the church. If Moody tries to leave, stop
him."

"Sure, Chief, but—"

"Tell him anything," Olivera broke in, "tell him the
county's set up a road block." Olivera grabbed his hat
and briefcase. "You stay out there, and I'll meet you soon
as I can."

With those quick instructions, Olivera rushed out
the door. There was no time to think, but he *did* think,
his reflections as jumbled as the thoughts of a drowning
man. His *map*, his *idea* of the crime, his ponderous
examination of people of interest—had any of it actually
led to the solution? What, in reality, had solved the
murder of Sister Clare? The answer came on the heels of
the question. "Mosey Frye," he sputtered, pounding the

steering wheel. Loath as he was to admit it, he had no word for the role she'd performed in three investigations, if not for "closer." In the blink of an eye, she'd spotted the missing piece, the empty space on his sketch of the crime scene where a shovel ought to have been. He should have thanked her wholeheartedly but hadn't. Envy had stood in the way. Instead of expressing his appreciation, he'd dismissed her quite abruptly.

His head drooped forward, and, for a second, he was a kid again, standing in front of his mother, ashamed of himself. As he pushed through the courthouse door, he set his reflections aside, then placed his evidence before the judge and got the arrest warrant he'd come for.

Judge Hendricks, robed and white haired, picked up his cane and accompanied him down the hall to the main door. "Gus, let's try to avoid a trial on this one if we can."

"Why do you say that, Judge?"

"Father Moody, my God, man. This is going to hit the community, well, I don't have to tell *you*, or maybe I do—how long you been here?"

"A year."

"So, maybe you don't know."

"Know what?"

"Melvin Moody is a local man. Grew up here. Dirt poor family. An orphan, raised by his older brothers. The only one of the bunch to make anything of himself."

"You think Arnold Bilyeu paid him to cover up the murder of Eugene Brown?"

"If Bilyeu had the money, I wouldn't put it past him. Arnold Bilyeu was the dregs of a high standing family. Jake made a fortune, and Arnold lost it, died a ruined man. Squandered everything he had except Larkspur."

"How'd he hang on to the land?"

"He died, that's how."

"Hmm."

He rested his hand on Olivera's shoulder and pushed open the door with his cane. "You remember what I'm telling you."

"I'll do my best."

On the way to St. Mary's, Olivera reviewed the case in his mind in light of what the judge had said. If the case *did* go to trial, was there any chance Moody might get off? He was certain he'd killed Ninon—well, maybe not *certain*. The physical evidence was damning enough. Still, he had to admit it wasn't incontrovertible. Short of a confession, he had no way of knowing for sure *who* killed Ninon. Moody could have come along after she was killed, picked up the bloody shovel... But, if he was innocent, why wouldn't he have said that, explained the whole situation? To avoid raising suspicion? Possibly.

The burning question remained unanswered: if he'd killed her, *why* had he killed her? It was unfathomable that a rural priest, residing for years in close proximity to a reclusive nun, would suddenly have taken a dagger—belonging to *her* not him, a fact which likely eliminated premeditation—and drive it into her abdomen, draining the life out of her with one powerful thrust.

Besides all that, the crime scene implied that the assailant might have preferred *not* to kill his victim. There weren't any signs of rage, such as repeated stabbings. It was more probable, he thought, he'd killed out of necessity. He'd killed her because he *had* to.

He set aside the actual event and returned to the incidents that preceded the crime—DeGroat's visit to the hermitage closely followed by Ninon's unearthing of the heirlooms. If Father Moody had seen her digging, as he'd claimed he had, he might also have seen the trunk and its contents. The sight of the dagger might have called up horrific memories from his youth when, orphaned and poor, he'd become involved in a heinous crime, not as instigator but, rather, as accomplice to his boss, Ninon's father.

Then what? An exchange must have ensued between Moody and Ninon. Would he have said—? Would she have volunteered—? Olivera couldn't reconstruct with any degree of certainty the exchange of accusations, pleas, excuses that may or may not have passed between them. Yet he strongly sensed that, by one path or another, they'd returned to the original crime scene and, finding themselves at cross purposes, had been swept up in a current of violence more powerful than they. The shadow of a formidable master, Arnold Bilyeu, loomed over them. And as Ninon tried desperately to extricate herself from her father's influence and evil, Moody, a condemned man in his own mind, had blocked her. But why?—when he could have confessed, allowing it all to come out. Undeniably, that would have been the better course, the more ethical course. So why, then? Pride? Loss of face? Could such things matter to a priest?

Olivera stopped at the four-way crossing and looked both ways before turning onto the gravel road that led to the church. He was somewhat satisfied with his *idea* of the crime, but would he be able to convince a prosecutor? Would the physical evidence be enough? He somehow doubted that it would, especially if Moody insisted on his innocence, claimed he knew nothing of either crime. He sighed heavily and paused before opening the car door. In that brief pause, he remembered Judge Hendricks's apprehension. The judge had a point. If the case *did* go to trial, its weaker elements could easily spark dissension among the citizenry. Some would cling to Moody's innocence, while others would swear to his guilt. Would the prosecutor be able to prove beyond a shadow of doubt *who* killed Ninon, or Eugene Brown, for that matter? The more he pondered, the more uncertain he became.

He spotted Springer and Reagan in the police van and assumed Moody was in the church. He pulled up and rolled down the window. "Did you speak to Moody?"

"No, Chief, and if he's in there, he's not budging."

"I'll go in the front door. Reagan, you come with me. Springer, you go around back. Hold tight in case he makes a run for it. I don't think he will, but you never know."

Olivera parked, got out, and he and Reagan entered the foyer. "Father Moody," Olivera called out, then tapped lightly on the office door.

No one answered.

He tried the knob but the door was locked. "Father Moody, Lieutenant Olivera here. Open the door, please." He turned to Reagan and, lowering his voice, said, "Go around to the back and see if Springer has seen anything, then come back here."

In minutes, the two officers returned.

"I know he's in there," Olivera said. "We may have to break down the door, but first, Springer..." He lowered his voice again. "There's a small window on the side of the church just past the front wall. See if you can see anything."

Springer left the foyer, and Olivera knocked again. "Father Moody, I have a warrant for your arrest. Open up."

In an instant, Springer was back at the entrance.

"What?" Olivera said.

Springer removed his hat and, in hang-jawed shock, leaned against the doorframe. "He's hanged himself, Chief."

While Olivera called Dr. McGinnis, the officers loosened the door hinges, allowing entrance to the dead priest's office. The body hung from a beam. The bench, where he and Moody had set their glasses, lay on its side below the dead man's feet. Shards of broken glass caught the radiance of the afternoon sun and scattered it across the stucco walls of the cubicle.

Chapter Twenty-Eight

Monday, September 28, night
Home of Lieutenant Olivera

The night following the discovery of Moody's body, the case began to unravel, maybe not in the public eye but most definitely in the judicious mind's eye of Gus Olivera.

Once McGinnis had left the crime scene to return to the morgue, he, Springer, and Reagan had headed back to the station. Then Olivera, on his way home, stopped by the courthouse to talk to Judge Hendricks. There wouldn't be a trial, given that the prime suspect was dead. An inquest, however, might be in order. They agreed to delay a decision till after the postmortem.

Having arrived home late and exhausted, Olivera went straight to bed. During the frenetic week that preceded Moody's death, he had spent his time gathering information, running from one place to the next—the station, the morgue, the courthouse, the law firm, the Tavernette, even Nadia Abboud's antique shop. In focusing his attention on *what was going on*, however, he'd failed to take sufficient note of *what went on*. And now that he'd solved the case, his thoughts shifted toward the latter. What did the case look like now, in light of his findings?

He rolled from his damp pillow onto the cool, satiny

smoothness of the pillow next to his. He closed his eyes and tried to sleep. He couldn't. Two grim images kept swapping off in his mind: first, Moody's fingerprints in the victim's blood, identical, if slightly distorted, to the prints Springer had taken the day after Sister Clare's murder; then, the lifeless body of the alleged assailant, still in primary flaccidity when Springer and Reagan had lowered it onto the stretcher. McGinnis said he'd been dead maybe an hour, even though in the ambient heat the eyelids, jaw, and neck had begun to stiffen. Her photographs would likely establish certain vital facts related to the cause of death. But in Olivera's mind, it was the broken glass strewn across the rough pine floor, the musty smell of the room, and the overturned bench at the suicide's feet that spoke to the agony of the priest's final moments.

He would have to base his conclusions on that same evidence: prints in the victim's blood, the suspect's death by suicide. But between these poles of relative certainty lay a jumble of loose ends. The entire matter had come to an abrupt halt, finished before he was ready for it to be. He rolled back over and switched on the light.

"Waaanh," came a cry from the foot of the bed.

"Oh, Milly, you can't sleep either? We know who killed your momma, at least we think we know." He sat up, slipped his feet into his house shoes. "Father Moody. Can you believe it? He's dead. Hanged himself. No trial. An inquest, maybe." He put on his robe and, cradling the small cat in one arm, shuffled to the kitchen. "Let's have a cup of chamomile—what do you say?" He dropped her onto her cushion. "Stay right there. Tea is on its way."

He put the kettle on, and with Milly at his heels, he headed for the porch. It was dark, and there wasn't any light coming from the neighboring houses except for the gas lantern in the adjacent yard. There was little sound, other than the relentless whirring of air conditioners. Even the tree frogs were silent. The blooming nightshade sent invisible puffs of essence across the porch. He breathed deep and lay down on the lounge chair to wait for the water to boil.

It was nearly October now. A week had passed since Sister Clare's murder on September 22, the first day of fall. He thought about that late afternoon when he'd gotten the call from Frank Jr., who'd stammered his request in monosyllables: *Get here quick as you can.* A short conversation with Eads McGinnis had followed. He and Springer had sped to St. Mary's from across town. He recalled their arrival, their scrutiny of the crime scene, and, later, the strange airy cross of airplane exhaust over the spot where the body had lain.

His follow-up was well planned. He'd taken all the proper steps. But now that the investigation was over, he realized that while he'd followed the story fairly well, the "characters"... He wished he'd gotten to know them better. To him, they were little more than stick figures on a stage: Ninon Bilyeu, Eugene Brown, Father Moody, Mannix, the deceased's distant cousins. Not even the Fergusons, whom he'd known previous to the incident, were fully fleshed out in his mind. This distressed him, especially in regard to Moody. He'd spoken with him briefly three times: the day of the murder, the following morning at the station, and a short while before he'd hanged himself. He was pretty sure, though not entirely, that Moody was guilty of at least one murder. His role in Brown's death seemed less certain. Maybe he *did* kill Brown, but more likely, he'd assisted the real culprit,

Ninon's father. But, then, if his role in the murder was minor, why would he have killed to keep the crime from coming out?

The whistle blew. He walked quickly to the kitchen, poured water over the tea bag, and returned to the porch.

He had nothing conclusive on either of them, Arnold Bilyeu or Moody, and only by hearsay had he learned of what Ninon had told her confessor. Except for the prints in her blood, the evidence was pretty thin in both cases. The scenarios he'd devised were based largely on supposition. For lack of sufficient evidence and without an eyewitness to either stabbing, his accounts of the fatal events were, in essence, imaginary. He knew nothing of the words spoken, the heated exchanges that must have occurred prior to the dreadful plunge of the dagger. He'd worked with the pieces of the puzzle he knew, moving them around, trying to understand how one might act on another. But these pieces, he had to admit, were only the ones *he knew*. What about the *invisible* ones? The ones that were there, but he, for the life of him, couldn't see.

The disagreeable little game he'd been playing hadn't gotten him very far. He might have won, if not for the prime suspect's final move. Now he'd have to settle for less than a win. He wondered what it would take to round out his idea of the crime.

He sipped his chamomile and thought. Yes, a confrontation with Moody could have been crucial. Would he have confessed, if faced with the evidence against him? Olivera wanted to know not only if he'd done it but *how* he could have brought himself to murder a defenseless eremitic nun. That was the big stumbling block. He couldn't get past it.

Olivera was angry. Of course, he was. No one was

going to be held accountable. There wouldn't be any justice for Sister Clare or Eugene Brown. An old saying came to mind, something he'd heard his father say. *Muerto el perro, se acabó la rabia.* There was no good way to say it in English: *When the dog dies, rabies dies with him.* But in Spanish the words "rabies" and "rage" were the same. The saying didn't translate, not fully. Moody was dead, but, in spite of that, Olivera's anger against him lingered.

Clearly, accountability was off the table. But there was something else gnawing at him. Melvin Moody and Father Galloway, his prime suspect in the Santa Clara stranglings, seemed as far apart as their respective dioceses. He could imagine that Galloway had strangled those women. He was a stern, powerful man, ambitious, too. Moody, to the contrary, was a humble country priest. If Ninon had threatened to reveal his role in Brown's murder, would he have killed her to shut her up? Doubt lingered and would continue to linger unless someone could tell him something more about the man's character. Someone who had known him, known him well for a long time. It suddenly came to him who that person might be: Monsignor Mannix. With Ninon and Moody dead, maybe Mannix would share, off the record, his own thoughts about the man, some frailty he'd observed that might have allowed him to commit such a horrific, impetuous act.

He set his cup in the sink, went back to bed, and slept till just past dawn. By nine o'clock, he was in Conakry, tapping on the door at the back corner of St. Patrick's.

"Lieutenant, I was expecting you," Mannix said. "Come in."

"Expecting me?" Olivera said.

"Yes, actually, I was. Have a seat. Can I offer you something…coffee?"

"I'll take a cup, if—"

"It's no trouble." He set down the cup he was holding and poured another. "You take anything in it?"

"Black's fine." He sat in the armchair and rested his hat on his knees.

"Yes, Lieutenant," Mannix handed him the cup, "I had an idea you might want to ask me about Melvin. You figure I would know, if anyone." He didn't seem upset at all. In fact, he looked relieved.

"So, Monsignor, *do you know*?"

"No, not if you're thinking in terms of a confession to murder. I have nothing to say on that count. But the man himself, well, I can see no harm in expressing an opinion, independent of anything he might have told me in confidence."

"Did you know him well?" Olivera sipped his coffee and held it in his hands, given there was nowhere to set it, no coffee table, no end table—just the monsignor's desk and the armchair.

"We weren't friends. Not really, but definitely more than acquaintances. When I came to St. Patrick's, Moody had already settled in at St. Mary of the Angels. But later on, I was told that the appointment hadn't gone through smoothly. Somebody in the Archbishop's office had voiced opposition."

Olivera was tempted to ask why, but he said nothing, his preference being to allow Mannix to follow the thread of his thoughts.

"I never broached the topic of church politics with Melvin. You, see, I came here from a very political diocese and was hoping to get away from all that. As you might imagine, politics as such doesn't amount to a hill of beans in a place like Conakry or Hembree."

"Now that you mention it, Monsignor, I suppose I have always assumed that. I mean, assumed a priest in an out of the way place would conform to a certain, well, uh, stereotype."

"Yes, an easy assumption. I suppose there are those who fit the stereotype, but, then, there are others who end up here or wherever for reasons other than humility or indifference to advancement."

Mannix poured himself a second cup. "Top that off for you, Lieutenant?"

"No, thanks, I'm good." He waited for Mannix to return to his bench, then said, "Was Father Moody in Hembree for some *other reason*?"

He nodded. "Yes, I believe he was."

"Did it have anything to do with Sister Clare?"

"No."

"Then what? I mean—" Olivera feared his question might have been too direct.

"*What*, you ask." Mannix got up and walked to the window. "If I had to be specific, I'd say he had certain attitudes that might have been tolerated around here. Well, some dioceses wouldn't have been so tolerant of his opinions. He had some fixed notions of what was what. You could say he hadn't changed much with the times." He remained staring out, as a person sometimes does when speaking an uncomfortable truth.

"Hadn't evolved, you mean."

Mannix glanced back at him but said nothing.

"I wouldn't suppose those opinions, as you say, would have anything to do with, uh, this outcome." Olivera got up and stood next to Mannix, hoping he would tell him more, something that would throw light on Moody's ability to commit murder.

"I read the piece in the paper." He motioned toward the *Gazette* that lay folded next to his laptop. "I know about the prints that were found on the shovel."

"Then you must wonder, as I do—"

"Of course, the insinuation is clear enough."

"Yes and no," Olivera said. "To me, his suicide is even more suggestive."

"They are damning, taken together, aren't they?"

"But we can't know for sure—probably will never know—unless someone gives us something."

"I have nothing to give that would prove his guilt or innocence."

Olivera dropped his head. "I suppose, then, we'll never know. And it's a shame."

"What?"

"No justice for Sister Clare or Eugene Brown."

"If you mean in a court of law."

Olivera wasn't so bold as to say *what other kind of justice is there?* "Yes, as an officer of the law, I'd hoped to bring Sister Clare's assailant to justice and, if possible, Eugene Brown's."

"There were no other suspects?"

"No, no one with motive and opportunity. The evidence I was able to gather pointed to Moody."

"There's a final justice…beyond the courts."

He thought Mannix might say something like that, and, in this instance, he begrudged him his fortress in religion. The two men sat uncomfortably for a moment. "I understand, Monsignor, that you'll be delivering the eulogies for Sister Clare and Father Moody."

"Yes, that's right."

Olivera stood and shook Mannix's hand. "I wish you well with that."

He hadn't gotten all of the answers he'd come for, but what he'd gotten would have to be enough.

Epilogue

Since Lieutenant Gustavo Olivera has passed to me, Anne Moseby Frye, the task of recounting in summary fashion the events that transpired in Hembree, Arkansas, in the days that followed the deaths of Sister Clare and Father Moody, I will begin by mentioning in passing that, as the old saying goes, *it is an ill wind that blows no good*. As distressing as, indeed, was the occasion, all the funeral parlors and florists in the vicinity experienced a surge in business never before known in these parts. Wreaths and floral sprays arrived from as far away as Pine Bluff and Helena, some in the shape of a heart or cross, some with ribbons that bore witness to the high esteem in which the deceased were held. Gray's Funeral Home embalmed and displayed the bodies in adjacent rooms. The remains of Eugene Brown, however, were sent to Memphis for cremation, where, as a result of the persistence of the coroner, Dr. Eads McGinnis, dental records surfaced identifying the John Doe skeleton as the long missing brother of T. Patrick Brown. More meaningful in some respects, McGinnis was able to locate Brown's widow and sons, greatly distraught and yet relieved to know at last the whereabouts of their beloved husband and father, who, in 1970, at a time when his children were not quite grown, had departed Memphis never to return. Mrs. Rosalind Brown and her sons along with their wives and children came to

Hembree the morning of the funeral, which was the second of three that took place in a week's time at St. Mary of the Angels Catholic Church, all conducted by Monsignor Mannix of Conakry.

Mr. A. B. Bilyeu and Mr. Cecil DeGroat extended their stay in Hembree by several days, so as to attend the funeral mass of their cousin, who, eulogized by the monsignor, her long-time confessor and friend, was described as a simple, unaffected woman, who, like her namesake St. Clare of Assisi, had rejected wealth and privilege for a life of prayer and contemplation. Two days later, the Browns and Smileys, along with the better part of the Eastside citizenry and other Hembreeites who chose to honor in death a man few had known in life, gathered at the same church to lay to rest the ashes of Eugene Brown. T. Patrick Brown arrived in a wheelchair pushed by his nephews, Eli and Pat, in whose eyes he glimpsed again the stars that he, as a boy, had seen in the eyes of his older brother.

The next day, the priest of St. Mary's was buried in the small cemetery beside the church; and despite the ignominious complexities of his life and death, streams of parishioners entered the sanctuary to pay their respects to the man who, from a young age to his death, had faithfully ministered to their spiritual needs.

A. B. Bilyeu, Cecil DeGroat, his sister Emma— who, expecting a baby was unable to travel to Hembree for the funeral or the reading of the will—and Rafael de Lobos inherited what remained of the Hembree Bilyeu estate. As dictated by the will, Bilyeu and DeGroat became the managers of Larkspur and, with the technical support of Blanchard College, would restore the old main house, the summer house, and several small buildings where those who worked the land had been allowed to live in partial payment for their labor. Lobos departed Hembree with the two dueling pistols and the odious bejeweled dagger, heirlooms that the church declared rightfully his, despite the final wishes of the deceased nun. The apothecary, which linked the early Bilyeus to the deaths of their house servants, was placed in the Apothecary Museum in New Orleans.

An autopsy convinced Dr. McGinnis to record Father Moody's cause of death as suicide. Lieutenant Olivera, however, hasn't established in his own mind the priest's definitive culpability in any one of three acts of violence. Evidence pointed to Moody's involvement in the murders of Brown and Ninon Bilyeu. Yet, in the eyes of the law, he went to his grave *not guilty*, since he neither confessed nor went to trial. His state of mind at the time of his suicide remained unknown, and that, together with the regrettable circumstances of his youth, compelled the diocese to allow for a funeral mass and burial in hallowed ground.

Neither Hershel Bilyeu, his wife Fernanda de Lobos, nor their great-grandson Arnold, all deceased, could be brought to justice for their alleged crimes against African Americans in New Orleans and Hembree, crimes that occurred, respectively, in 1860 and more than a hundred years thereafter. Though nothing much was said about it at the time, at least not publicly, the significance of the death of Eugene Brown was not lost on Nadia Abboud, Saffron Smiley, or myself. With the details supplied by my dear friend Nadia, who, as I have often said, stands toe to toe with history, we felt as if we had stepped back into the annals of Hembree labor relations, where conflicts between sharecroppers and the cotton elite—

planters, brokers, bankers—had been recorded not boldly but in delible ink that, over time, left little more than a smudge on the public consciousness. I wish I could say we did something important to remedy the blur by illuminating that dark period. The entire town, indeed, the whole state, ought to know what transpired in the years after World War I, when African American farm laborers briefly asserted their will in hopes of securing for themselves what was rightfully theirs. We've left it for others to assume that important task. We did, however, spread the message among all who would listen, mainly our families and friends. I am also glad to report that, once the old Bilyeu place was up and running again and the buildings were restored—making Larkspur one of a handful of restored plantations on the Arkansas side of the Mississippi River—a plaque was placed on the summer house in memory of Eugene Brown. It reads: "In loving memory of Eugene Brown, 1915-1970. The son of sharecroppers, he lived and worked at Larkspur Plantation and was instrumental in organizing African American farm laborers. Later, he moved to Memphis, where he realized his dream of becoming a musician. In 1970, he met his death under mysterious circumstances, and on September 23, 2009, his skeletal remains were discovered in the cistern of the old overseer's house at Larkspur, later known as the Summer House. With this plaque, the owners of Larkspur and the Hembree community mark his passing and honor his participation in efforts to inspire solidarity among those who toiled the land for meager compensation."

Anne Moseby Frye
September 1, 2012

A word about the author...

Kay Pritchett was born and bred in Greenville, Mississippi, and attended Millsaps College in Jackson. She completed her education at the University of North Carolina, Chapel Hill, where she received her doctorate in Spanish Literature. After a long stint in Spain, she accepted an offer at the University of Arkansas and, at retirement in 2016, delved fully into fiction writing. *Murder in High Cotton* (The Wild Rose Press, 2022), inspired by memories of the Delta, anthologizes her first three short mystery novels. Book #4 in the series, *The Summer House at Larkspur* is her first full-length novel. She lives in Fayetteville, Arkansas, with her husband Christopher J. Huggard.

Thank you for purchasing
this publication of The Wild Rose Press, Inc.

For questions or more information
contact us at
info@thewildrosepress.com.

The Wild Rose Press, Inc.
www.thewildrosepress.com